About the Author

Janet lives with her long-suffering partner of thirty-five years, Alex, in Cannock, Staffordshire. She has a son, Kevin, and two grandchildren, Tom and Grace. Janet is a retired newspaper reporter/college lecturer in English and Creative Writing.

She runs a charity, Paul's Fun Fund, which raises money for leukaemia research as a tribute to her eldest son Paul, who lost his battle with the disease in 2011 at the age of thirty-seven.

Janet loves rock music and writing. The book is largely based on the author's real experiences. Readers can decide which parts are true, which are embellished – and which are wishful thinking.

Mistress Magic

Janet Lee

Mistress Magic

Olympia Publishers

London

www.olympiapublishers.com
OLYMPIA PAPERBACK EDITION

A CIP catalogue record for this title is
available from the British Library.

ISBN: 978-1-78830-066-7

This is a work of fiction.
Names, characters, places and incidents originate from the writer's
imagination. Any resemblance to actual persons, living or dead, is purely
coincidental.

First Published in 2018

Olympia Publishers
60 Cannon Street
London
EC4N 6NP

Printed in Great Britain

Dedication

Dedicated to my gorgeous, energetic son Kevin, who's always on the go – hence his nickname 'Revin'. ('Daddy Cool' to his kids Tom and Grace)

Acknowledgments

Thank you, guys.

Thank you from the bottom of my heart to Alex (rhythm guitar), Andy (drummer) and Derek (lead guitar) for believing in me for as long as you did. Without you all I would never have known the extraordinary, wonderful and terrifying experience of singing in a rock band.

Chapter One

It was enough to make Dr Johnson turn in his grave – his beloved city turned into a laughing stock, a fiasco.

There are those who maintain the famous son of Lichfield in Staffordshire liked a laugh. He is credited with writing the first ever English dictionary and it is said there are some very funny entries.

Lord knows he would need his sense of humour. Contending with tourists was one thing. Having his precious city ridiculed for being at the centre of strange goings-on was quite another.

Events unfolded in the early 1980s and the respectable cathedral city was about to be shaken to its ancient foundations.

The Arts Centre, an odd combination of scruffiness and picturesque charm, nestled on the edge of Minster Pool. It could hold its own among the most romantic of European locations. Swans glided effortlessly by, mature trees overhung the pool as if in deference to the camera. The cathedral posed majestically and obligingly for the photographer. A more serene scene would be hard to find.

Bang! Crash! Smash! Clang!

Cymbals scattered everywhere. Drums careered across the Arts Centre floor.

"Shit!" yelled Riff, flame-haired wild man of the latest bunch of local 'musicians' to drag their scruffy asses to the Arts Centre.

'Arts Centre' it may have been called, but you really should have been there on a Friday night—

Riff was a member of a local rock band with big ideas. They were original, the best and were going to take the world by storm (in their opinion). And even after just a few rehearsals, they told anyone who would listen that this would be so.

Riff rounded up his errant cymbals, his tools of trade, from the dusty floor.

Des, an electric performer on (electric) guitar but short fused on a few internal light bulbs 'upstairs', was dragging a heavy amplifier across the newly refurbished wooden floor, gouging out deep scratch marks in the woodwork. That floor was the pride and joy of the devoted caretaker.

A more poignant contrast it would be hard to find. Outside, the Arts Centre was tranquil. Inside, on this Sunday afternoon, five members of a band collaborated on a project which, unknown to them at the time, would put Staffordshire on the map for all the wrong reasons.

Lead singer Janine, barely five feet tall, was thirty-one years old, divorced with two kids. She saw the band as her last shot as she was already the wrong side of thirty, a way out of drudgery. She was a peculiar mix of personality: intelligent, yet happiest when with non intellectuals; an English teacher at the nearby prestigious King Edward VI school by day – a leather-clad, mini-skirted, wannabe rock singer at night. She actually got a kick out tearing out of school in her beaten up MG BGT and as soon as she got home, throwing off her sensible skirt and blouse and pulling on her short leather mini and thigh-length leather boots. She found it helped to wear her stage gear even on the way to rehearsals. It made her feel less 'housewife-ly'.

Sons Paul and Lucas were quite used to Mummy standing sidewise in front of the mirror cursing her non-existent 'fat' tummy as she flattened down the front of the leather mini and checked the buttons were secure on the leather waistcoat (with nothing underneath). In their household this was the norm.

Despite her raunchy image, flowing dyed blonde locks and piercing green eyes Janine was a devoted mum. A divorcee, she shared her life with her partner, rhythm guitarist Alex, a skinny painter and decorator with long black hair. Patient and kind, he provided for all her needs – musically and sexually. They were an irreverent couple, but fiercely loyal. And of necessity they both worked hard to pay the bills.

When they weren't trying to be rock stars there was a sense of domesticity. He fixed her kids' toys when they broke and cleaned their shoes ready for school.

The boys were eight and six years old when Janine and Alex first got together, so by the time they were ten and thirteen they were used to a rock lifestyle.

They all squashed into a tiny, rented, two-bed flat which they turned into a home full of laughter and rock music.

"For Christ's sake, Des, watch the bloody floor!" Alex yelled.

Janine's toy boy he may have been, but in many ways he was older than his twenty-four years. Alex was the practical member of the band, the one who was forever fixing and soldering.

Even now he tried to cover over the scratch marks in the floor as best he could while hapless Des looked on. Blond and blue eyed Des may have been, but that was no guarantee of success with women – and his love life was little short of a disaster. He grumbled that in one particular sexual escapade the woman never even kissed him. Still, he entertained the band members with his self-effacing stories.

Drummer Riff had no such problems where women were concerned. He was an extrovert with long hair and tassels tied around his arms. Girls loved him. Current girlfriend Sam, petite and well spoken, struggled across the floor with the drum kit. How her parents must have despaired.

Bass player Pete arrived late as usual, his lanky, long locks hiding his expression. Did he really want to be here at all? Would he rather be sitting at home on a Sunday afternoon watching TV? This was one of three weekly rehearsals – and he was the only member of the band who saw this as a chore.

Somehow, this motley crew (whose heroes included Motley Crue) assembled themselves every Sunday afternoon at the Arts Centre to rehearse. Janine's kids, if they weren't staying with her ex, would accompany them.

It was only after a few weeks of rehearsals that the band's name was formed – and the choice should have been obvious all along. As lead singer, and with a degree education behind her, Janine paraded in a mortar board and gown for a band photo shoot. Everyone thought it was funny to have a teacher wearing leather mini and waistcoat with thigh-length boots clearly visible under the gown. They liked the implied two finger salute, an affront to authority.

And so Mistress was born – with all its connotations.

Chapter Two

Despite being shattered by the end of each working day, Alex and Janine held 'open house' to all and sundry at their meagre flat.

Riff, who actually lived with his parents in a luxurious house in a posh area near Lichfield, seemed to prefer spending his evenings talking rock music and being interrupted by Janine's kids, who demanded attention even after bed time.

Despite the wild man exterior Riff was actually a kind person, even giving the kids some of his long-forgotten toys which he found in the attic at home.

Ironically, it was Des, the least academic, who was the most financially secure. While Alex and Janine lurched from one rent month to another, Des's family puzzled over which Rolls Royce they would drive that day. As market traders in a nearby city they had done more than OK for themselves.

Des was particularly important to the band because as well as being a naturally brilliant guitarist he became its chief financier of equipment.

Alex, the perfectionist, had rehearsed the band almost to the point where they never wanted to hear their own songs again. But on the upside, they could perform almost automatically and were all finely tuned. It was one and a half years before he decided they were ready to perform. Having been in bands before, with varying degrees of success, he was determined that this one would hit the ground running.

Every waking minute, every member of the band (except the reluctant bass player) went over and over the songs in their heads, dreaming of stardom – whether they were awake or asleep. In addition to three rehearsals a week they went over and over their parts at home, in the car, any place, any time.

Janine's ex had told her the only way she would be on a stage would be to 'sweep it' – a comment that stung and made her all the more determined to prove him wrong.

At last the first gig was arranged: it was to be on 'safe ground' at a pub in Birmingham called the Toby Jug which was run by a friend of Janine's.

There was only a small crowd even though Alex and Janine had personally gone around the district a week before and plastered Mistress posters everywhere – incurring the wrath of the local council.

Riff's girlfriend had offered to operate the mixing desk. And whatever happened, the band could not be accused of being under rehearsed.

The night before the gig Alex and Janine had the most desperate impromptu sex session across the washing machine. She had put on her stage gear to psyche herself up for the following night. Alex was only too willing to do anything that took his mind off the tedium of painting and decorating in the morning. Their tiny first floor flat had a long narrow hall – so narrow that it was almost impossible to walk past each other without physically touching – so that's what they often did. And, well, one thing usually led to another.

Despite wanting this band desperately, Janine wondered what on earth she was doing. Rehearsals were one thing; a performance was another. In the event the gig was more than they could have hoped for. Des was surrounded by impressed guys in the audience afterwards and one enthusiastic young woman came up to Janine and told her, "You're going to be big, really big. I can feel it in my bones!"

What an accolade and Janine believed it. The band wanted more than anything for the prediction to come true, but on their own terms.

At the next gig, the City Frog pub in Lichfield, Janine dreaded the thought that some of her students might be in the audience. A large bottle of Martini Rosso seemed to put paid to her nerves that night.

The City Frog gig turned out to be unremarkable. Despite pre advertising the pub was not packed out and in all honesty the band did not go down a storm – which was a huge disappointment after the Toby Jug performance which lulled the band into a false sense of anything being possible. Another bottle of Martini helped to get rid of the disappointment.

As the band packed away their equipment Riff decided he would chase Janine around the pub with a vibrator which he had found on Cannock Chase, a local beauty spot where he worked as a forest ranger. Janine squealed and ran out of genuine revulsion, but couldn't help laughing at the ridiculousness of the situation. It was all part of the crazy band/family life which made her feel a genuine affection.

Riff and Janine were perhaps the closest in the band, possibly because they were most vain so spent a lot of time preening themselves and each other.

As the band took on more gigs at various less than salubrious venues, they frequently spent time getting changed into their stage gear in the back of the band's Sherpa van. There was a mutual understanding that they would avert their eyes during part of the undignified, indelicate process. Part of the van's registration number was MHL - which stood for Mistress Has Landed as far as the band was concerned.

Oddly, though there was much love and respect between band members this was not reflected in the songs. Janine was the main lyric writer, but Des also occasionally came up with inspired lyrics of his own.

Janine had a pathological hatred of same-y old love songs. Instead she wrote about space, religion, escaped convicts, Knights of the Round Table, things that went bump in the night – ANYTHING except love.

She would listen intently to Alex or Des churning out riffs haphazardly and would know instantly if she heard something that could be built into a song. This often caused huge arguments between Janine and Alex.

"Play that bit again! Play that bit again! No – not like that - like you just played it!"

And there would be numerous arguments along the lines of, "That IS how I played it!"

"No it isn't! Oh, give me the damn guitar. I'll play it myself!"

Some of the best songs came about during jam sessions and frustrated arguments at the flat. And the band members tolerated having to 'play it again, play it again, play it again' interminably until Jan had the mood of the song and the lyrics worked out.

The most difficult was a song called XLR8 – which was the word 'accelerate' getting faster and faster. That took some doing.

On one particular drink-fuelled night Alex got so carried away, he decided to set up his guitar and amplifier outdoors in the car park – at midnight. He struck up a chord and the whole sound seemed to reverberate around the neighbourhood. A couple of lads passing by were convinced he must be on drugs and told him, "Mate, you're gonna get arrested."

But Alex played on undeterred, really getting into his solo lead break. It was only when a man, clearly annoyed, came down the road in his pyjamas that he conceded it was clearly time to stop. Never mind, Alex and his band would have ample opportunity to create a stir in ways they couldn't have imagined.

Chapter Three

News of the band had started to filter through. The local newspaper came out to watch a rehearsal session, interview the band and carry out a photo shoot for their regular 'Sounds' music column.

Janine was flicking through the paper trying to find the Sounds column when it was printed the following week. She couldn't find the article so, thinking she had missed it somehow, started to search again. There was an 'Oh My God' moment when she found the picture and article. She had not even considered it might go front page so had not bothered looking there first time round.

But there she was on the front page – in leather mini – perched on top of a beer barrel in all her glory. Somehow, she had convinced herself that none of her students would notice an article in the Sounds column. They sure as hell would notice this.

The next day she skulked into a class of expectant – sixteen-year-olds.

"Miss—" one of them said. And Janine noticed the article placed neatly on her desk. The secret was out.

But it was not only the students who noticed. A female singer fronting a rock band was an unusual combination and was a draw – especially wearing that attire – so gradually the gigs started to attract a bigger audience.

Confident though the band's musicians were of their ability, the same could not be said of their lead singer. She looked great, but could she carry it off 'live' in bigger venues? The problem was the band played loud on stage and Janine struggled to hear herself, especially as she stood directly in front of the crashing, bashing drums of Riff. Des had come up with more cash to try and improve the on-stage monitors so Janine could hear herself.

The Arts Centre gig, on a hot July night, would be their biggest yet so they had planned to make it their best.

They had enlisted the help of a lights guy called Danny and asked if he would attend one of their rehearsals so he would know the songs. They figured if he had heard the songs he would know what atmosphere to create with the lights. He was a kind of geeky dude, not one to show emotion or excitement. Having operated the lights for loads of bands he'd seen it all anyway. This was his living and actually he now found it quite a bore.

He did attend a rehearsal, but it was clear he was there under duress. Who did this band think they were? Didn't they know he'd done the lights for countless bands? He KNEW what he was doing. He didn't need a rehearsal.

Janine's kids were allowed to sit at the front, but were under strict instructions not to call out 'Mummy' during the gig, which would ruin any 'street cred'.

"Now, if Mummy swears, that doesn't mean you can," they were told. "It's just an act, remember, not really Mummy. It's not nice to swear in real life."

And so, the kids sat waiting in anticipation for 'Mistress not mummy' to take to the stage.

The backdrop, made by a friend of a friend seamstress, was in place. It was a huge, black heavy curtain with 'Mistress' in gothic writing in red across it.

Janine was really scared. Half of Lichfield seemed to have crammed into the Arts Centre and she knew loads of the people in the audience, many of them in bands themselves. Playing before strangers was fine, but proving yourself in front of your contemporaries was something else.

Amongst the crowd were those Janine called the 'reverse snobs'. They dressed down deliberately even though their parents could afford to buy them all the latest designer gear.

Disregarding all the advice about alcohol being bad for your voice, more Martini helped to blot out/blotto the nerves. Meantime, Alex was throwing up in the loo in the area that masqueraded as a changing room.

Riff jogged on the spot like a boxer in training for his first bout and twiddled with his multi coloured streamers dangling from his wrist.

Des ran his fingers up and down his flying V guitar like there was no tomorrow. It was those flying fingers that got him the job in the first place. At the audition at Janine and Alex's flat he had only wailed out a few notes and they said, 'You're hired'. Des was the undisputed star of the band.

The bass player looked bored stiff.

The lights went down.

The intro tape played – a dramatic orchestral piece, the theme tune to a popular sci fi show at the time called *V.*

Even years later the sound of that tune was enough to make Janine's stomach lurch in anxiety.

As the intro tape played the band members groped their way onto the stage in the darkness, Janine standing with her back to the audience – her bum in black leather mini not quite visible.

The intro tape had been carefully doctored so that as it built up, the sound of a helicopter gradually took over, roaring over the speakers until the power chords of *Space is Ace* rang out - and Janine turned round to face the audience and sing the first line.

The only way she could remember the start of each line was to think of the word 'Dowry' which was near enough: D O W R. 'R' was also for 'repeat' the first verse at the end of the song – except for the last line, which changed.

Janine was very proud of her 'space-y' words, the rhyme structure, the way she managed to wheedle in the words 'space is ace' at certain points; and the change of mood for the chorus, which was slow and sexy compared to the fast-moving, wordy verses. The technique of using a sudden ending to the song then straight into the next one always added to its drama.

Space is Ace

Driftin' through the timeless zone
Sixteen million miles from home
Friends and foes seem far away
Though space is ace I'd rather stay away

Out beyond the atmosphere
Asteroids and hemisphere
Galaxies and meteorites
Though space is ace I'd rather see the light

Chorus
I'm comin', from the sun.
I'm comin', with a calcium man.

Welcome to the space station
In suspended animation
Light years from my ma and pa
I never dreamt I'd get so far away

Rockets fuelled by technology
Philosophy, psychology.
Computers say 'have a nice day'
Passin' by the Milk Way-hey.

Repeat chorus

Driftin' through the timeless zone
Sixteen million miles from home
Friends and foes seem far away
Who is caring anyway-hey?
(Sudden ending)

Janine and Alex managed to catch a glance and a grin across the stage during the song – just a small moment – but it was one that spoke volumes. This was their biggest gig so far and it was going well. The look said, 'We did it. And Janine didn't just sweep the stage'.

The band went straight into XLR8 – the one that had taken so much working out that night in the flat trying to get the letters XLR8 to morph into 'accelerate' as they got faster – and to get it all to fit to the music.

XLR8

Dogs on my heels
Help me to hide
My head reels
Don't let them find me

I can hear the sound
Handcuffs round my wrist
Guns – and hounds
I only got my fists

Chorus
I'm on the run
I'm on the run
Gotta move, gotta go,

I'm on the run
I'm on the X, L, R, 8
X, L, R, 8
X, L R8 – XLR8 - ACCELERATE

Pains in my chest
Heart beats in my ears
Trying to catch my breath
Hair is streaked with tears
Stung by the rain
Stumble and fall
Cryin' out in pain
Trying to cross the wall
CHORUS

Janine put everything into that song and found extra inspiration from the extraordinary efforts of the lights man. As she sang the chorus the outline of a man, brilliant white, was projected around the hall – running round the top of the walls at breakneck speed. It was very impressive. Oh, the wonders of new technology.

There was a roar from the crowd at the end of the song, as much as for the lighting effects as for the band's performance, Janine thought.

Janine could hear the falsetto voices of Paul and Lucas cheering. She distinctly heard one of the little horrors shout, 'Mum', but didn't dare look at them.

The next song was *Angel Rock*. Alex, enjoying the limelight, took centre stage to bash out its distinctive, catchy riff.

Despite its religious overtones it was a catchy, laid back song with sweet verses followed by a belting chorus with simple lyrics – one of those just begging the audience to join in.

And the chorus gave Janine the opportunity to really exploit what she was best at – being sexy. She would slink to the stage floor, knowing full well her mini skirt would rise even higher. She would bounce erotically as she sang the evocative word 'high' in the chorus, play with it, sing it softly until it almost disappeared, appeal to the audience to join in.

Slowly, as the chorus built back up in volume, she would stand up little by little, clench her fists and raise her hands as the volume increased.

Then, and only then, as she dropped her hands sharply the band would come to an abrupt, well-rehearsed sudden halt. The effect brought a wall of appreciative sound from the audience. At such times Janine felt like a conductor in control of her orchestra, each member watching her every move.

The song told the story of an angel who went to heaven – only to discover there was no rock music there.

Janine had no idea how this song would change her life in just a few short weeks.

Angel Rock

There was an angel, knew him well
Went to heaven but found it hell
All he found were flowers and harps
Said: "Bugger this for a lark."

Then the Lord looked down from high
Saw him rockin' in the sky
Expelled him from that heavenly place
Gabriel left in disgrace

Chorus
So he packed his wings
Took all his things
Angel rockin' on high
So he packed his wings
Took all his things
Angel rockin' on high, high, high
High, high, high.

If music be the food of love
Someone please tell God above
To let the rockers in his space
To liven up that dreary place

See if you identify
With the feelings of this guy
If you do I'll guarantee
You identify with me

Chorus
Repeat chorus quietly (playing on the word 'high' at the
end)
(Let me hear ya) high, high, high
(Like a mountain) high, high, high
(I wanna hear ya) high, high, high
(Building to crescendo)

29

High high high.
High, high, high
(Sudden end)

The band performed eight songs that night, dripping wet with sweat, happy that their first major gig had gone down a storm. There was even a shout of, 'we love you' from someone in the crowd.

After the performance it was Des, of course, who was the centre of attention, surrounded again by musicians and groupies, while band members struggled to pack up the gear. Ask Des to change a plug and he was clueless, give him a guitar and he was priceless.

At the end of a gig Janine was 'one of the lads'. Despite her diminutive stature she was hurling amplifiers, speakers and cabs into the van like an all-in wrestler.

As she packed everything from the dressing room there was one item missing – her mini skirt. She'd swopped her skirt for jeans so she could get stuck in putting all the equipment away. God knows what is happening to my skirt right now, she shuddered. Then she cursed at the expense of having to buy a replacement.

Janine spotted Danny trying to weave his way around the loitering punters as he packed away his lighting gear.

She brushed past the crowds, ignoring the sexist banter.

"Thank you so much," Janine said to Danny, who looked a bit bemused by her enthusiasm.

"That's cool," came the reply.

But Janine persevered because she felt he deserved the praise.

"That running man! I didn't expect that! It was awesome. How on earth did you do that?"

"I didn't," he replied in a matter of fact tone, hardly looking at her.

The crowd was starting to disperse but Janine still had to shout to make herself heard as most were the worse for wear after their heavy drinking session.

"What do you mean, you didn't?" she shouted, conscious that she was now getting on his nerves. "Who else did then?"

"Dunno," came the reply – and he continued winding up his leads, uninterested.

Janine's eyes darted around the venue. There was no other lights guy.

Alex joined them and handed over Danny's fee.

"Brilliant running man. We'll use that again," Alex said.

"He said he didn't do it," Janine said.

Alex laughed, a touch sarcastically, as if she was stupid.

"'Course he did. Who else was doing the lights?"

"Ask him then," Janine insisted. And she couldn't understand why she had a sense of unease.

Alex sighed. "You did the running man thing, didn't you?" he askedDanny.

"No, mate," came the reply as he carried on dismantling the lights.

"What the—" Alex's words trailed off as he looked round, puzzled, then shrugged his shoulders.

"Well, whoever did it - great job," then he shuffled off to carry on loading up.

Janine knew him so well. She knew he wouldn't give the matter a second thought.

She looked around the hall. The floor was beer soaked, mixed with discarded plastic glasses and cigarette ends. There were a few punters left, but there were more outside than inside now. She could hear them singing drunkenly outside.

'Thank goodness the kids are being looked after in the lounge area', she thought to herself as she set off to pick them up.

"Great running man!" one of the stragglers shouted to her as he staggered off.

Janine forced an insincere smile and did a thumbs-up as if acknowledging the lighting effect was part of the performance.

But she hadn't a clue – and neither had anyone else, it seemed.

Chapter Four

Life was busy for Janine, even without being in a rock band. With two boys and a full time job it was a constant battle to keep on top of the domestic organised chaos. In most normal households when a cupboard door is opened the mum can pull out the vacuum or ironing board. In Janine's flat, when she opened a cupboard door, a forest of microphone stands toppled onto her before she could even reach the vacuum.

But it was while she performed her mundane chores that she had some of her best ideas. Like an inspirational light bulb switching on in her head, a song title or catchy phrase would pop in.

And people would constantly pop in to Janine's and Alex's flat, which was an open house. Male and female friends and band members became quite used to Janine standing in her knickers running the iron over her jeans - usually while she listened to rock music and got a real rhythm going with the iron.

On one Saturday afternoon Riff called round for a coffee – still dressed as a rock star even though he was off duty. He was in a good mood so Janine didn't want to spoil his good humour by bringing up the running man in their conversation. She joined him in light-hearted chat about how the gig went and after a while asked in the most casual way she could muster, "And where DID that running man come from?"

"Search me," Riff said. "Must've been someone in the audience with a projector," then carried on prattling as if it didn't matter.

That night, friends Nick and Fiona came round for their usual treat of Martini and music. Relaxed and happy, all four sprawled on the carpet eating nibbles, Alex idly strumming acoustic guitar. In a rare, pensive mood he was playing randomly, picking out subtle chord sequences instead of bashing out rock at ninety miles an hour.

Janine was his biggest fan and critic, so even when he played background music she was always 'tuning in', ever alert in case he came up with anything which could be turned into a song. Pen and paper was always at hand.

At times like these he had come up with some quite beautiful tunes. Janine had even turned one of them into a song about a picture on their lounge wall. Lovely, but far too 'nice-y nice-y' to be used in a Mistress set.

They loved that picture. It was a farm cottage on a hillside with gathering clouds in the distance and poppy petals blowing in the wind.

Poppies red and flying
Flying in the breeze
In the distance dark clouds
Hills and trees between
Cottages with thunder rooves
Tumbledown and worn

Ducks meandering round the farm
Looking all forlorn

But tonight he had come up with a dirge-like sequence of chords. It was so creepy it actually made Janine shudder.

"Don't like that one," she said, hoping he would stop. But Alex took another swig of Martini and persevered, creating ever more depressing sounds which seemed to go on forever. No-one else seemed to have noticed, but Janine felt the room change and become really oppressive. She was just about to get up and open a window when—

"Shit!" she yelled as the lights went out and there was an almighty bang from the opposite end of the lounge. "What the hell—"

Janine fumbled for the light switch and found it worked immediately.

When she looked for the source of the noise she felt the breath leave her body. She stared wide-eyed at a large framed picture which had fallen off the wall. But it was the way it had landed that gave her the creeps. It was standing bolt upright on the coffee table. And the force of the jolt had dislodged the pretty sunflower picture which she had bought from a charity shop. The glass front and the picture had fallen forward, revealing a hideous smiling clown behind it. What made the photo all the more horrible was the tears running down the clown's face.

Shaking, Janine got up and inspected the nail on the wall. It was still in position and not at all wobbly. There was no reason she could see for the picture to fall. God, how she hated those fashionable crying clown pictures.

She whirled round, desperately trying to sound light-hearted.

"That's your bloody fault. You and that bloody creepy music."

Everyone laughed as Janine dumped the clown in the bin and struggled to put the picture back together.

But Alex, bolstered by the Martini, was ready to hit back.

"It's you, you witch," he teased. "Whenever you're around electrical stuff doesn't work. Even the bloody supermarket till packs up when you're at the head of the queue."

Nick and Fiona joined in the teasing. They reminded her they'd once witnessed, one summer, a spark actually jump from Janine to Alex when she touched him.

"It was static, you morons!" she protested – though she knew perfectly well she was more 'live' than most. Even the shelves in the supermarket gave her a shock sometimes.

Alex's melancholy phase was now well and truly over and he started bashing out Status Quo riffs.

All was well – for now.

Chapter Five

Although Janine wrote about scary stuff sometimes she was actually very scared of anything remotely paranormal. She once went on an organised ghost hunt to a supposedly haunted pub, persuaded because it was a friend's birthday treat. She spent the hours after midnight silently praying that nothing would happen. It was OK to watch these things on TV. But for real? Forget it.

She never forgot a séance she took part in as a teenager. She was singing with a band even then. Janine and the four guys thought it would be a laugh during their caravan holiday to set up a ouija board. They supposedly contacted a Chinese man and everyone was laughing, each convinced one of the others was moving the glass around to the ridiculous responses. When they asked for one particular message, random nonsensical letters followed one after another. No-one could fathom out what the letters meant and everyone was genuinely puzzled – until Janine said, heart pounding, "Oh my God – V.E.L.L.Y.S.O.L.L.Y – it says 'Velly Solly'!"

It was a paranormal joke that genuinely no-one had understood at first. And it wasn't funny. It scared everyone out of their wits and they stopped messing straight away.

Janine wrote one particular song that acknowledged her fears, *Run and Hide*.

Run and Hide

Did you watch the late-night show?
Are you walkin' home alone?
Hearin' footsteps just behind.
Horror stories now crowd your mind.

Shapes on your bedroom wall
Look behind you and that ain't all
Fear the night it's so cold
Icy fingers around your soul.

Chorus
Run and, run and hide
Run and, run and hide
Run and, run and hide
Run and, run and hide

Janine was particularly proud of the *'icy fingers around your soul'* and she loved the chorus which was sung with the rest of the band members in harmony.

The next gig was looming. 'Looming' wasn't a word Janine usually associated with an upcoming gig. Normally she was excited. But this one was in a pub out of town with a completely new audience, about twenty miles away in a popular market town pub.

Friends Nick and Fiona had agreed to come along and do a basic light show for them, nothing fancy.

As the band tuned up at the gig Des managed to blow a fuse – a normal occurrence, that is, not by paranormal means. Alex quietly and patiently, through gritted teeth, replaced the fuse for him (again).

In fact this was how and why Janine had fallen for him in the first place. She remembered their first early rehearsals before Des was on the scene to splash the cash. Their equipment was battered and in constant need of repair so it was always breaking down. One day she watched as Alex knelt on the floor, hunched over the mass of wires, quietly soldering without losing his temper. And that was THE moment.

She often joked that one of her ex boyfriends was a brown-haired bass player in a band, her ex husband was a black-haired drummer, now she had a rhythm guitarist with long black hair – all she needed next was a lead singer with long blond hair and she'd have slept with a full band.

Alex took the comments all in his stride; she was all talk and no action. Despite the banter he knew that most teenagers these days had enjoyed more lovers than she had in a lifetime.

The gig kicked off as usual. XLR8 was in the middle of the set this time – and Janine breathed a huge sigh of relief to herself when nothing, absolutely nothing happened to unnerve her. She berated herself for being such a fool – and accepted what everyone had been telling her. The running man had been projected by someone in the audience.

They were loud tonight, so much so that the pub owner had to ask them to turn down a notch due to complaints from neighbours.

Des and Riff were in fine form. The bass player, usually quiet and reserved, almost shoved Janine off the stage with his uncharacteristic enthusiasm. It seemed he went into 'rock star' mode once the set started. Pity he couldn't have had some of that personality off stage, Janine thought. At times he took his on-stage enthusiasm too far, totally changing what they had rehearsed. Instead of bashing out the bass solidly in time with the drums as rehearsed, he would suddenly take it upon himself to start 'twiddly dee-ing' at break-neck speed up and down the fret – which annoyed the hell out of the band. That style of playing wasn't what the band was about, but he enjoyed his sneaked moments in the limelight.

Janine looked down at the gig list which was taped to the floor of the small stage.

Next up was her George Orwell-inspired tribute to his novel *1984*. She launched into the up tempo song in a good mood.

1984

It's 1984
They are knockin' on my door
Ain't as bad as the author said –
A time for all, a time to dread

And it's 1983
With optimism, that's me
Some predictions materialised
Orwell wasn't writing lies

Chorus
Silver trail lined with gold
There's a tale that I've been told
Followin' a yellow brick road
In no man's land, in no man's land, in no man's land

And it's 1985
When we're still alive
Perhaps we'll take a backward look
At a fairy tale, fiction book
Chorus

Though the verses had a meaning of sorts, the chorus was a creative combination of words which Janine simply liked the sound of – and which had a kind of *Wizard of Oz/Over the Rainbow* fantasy feel.

Two guys the worse for drink staggered to the front of the stage.

"Play *Satisfaction*!" one of them yelled.

"We don't do covers!" Janine managed to shout in his ear.

Covers? The whole point of Mistress was to perform their OWN songs.

Run and Hide was next on the list. They would just have to listen to that.

Janine put on her best creepy voice as she sang the opening lines: *Did you watch the late night show?*

She chuckled to herself as the two guys disappeared, disgruntled, into a fog of atmospheric smoke which crept from the stage and tumbled at ankle level into the crowd.

Hearin' footsteps just behind
Horror stories now crowd your mind

Janine savoured the moment. It was times like these that made it all worthwhile. She lost herself in the song as the mist swirled around her. She was loving it – until Alex bellowed in her ear, "You're singing flat!" which didn't do much for her confidence. It took all her resolve to keep her composure on stage.

The band finished with *Angel Rock*. Sudden ending, then, 'Thank you, goodnight'!'

The smoke was just about clearing as the band packed away after the gig. Just a few swirls remained at ground level, hampering Alex's attempts to unravel all the wires. He hated smoke machines, said they always made him cough, but the truth was more to do with his twenty-a-day smoking habit.

"Who the hell brought in the bloody smoke machine?" he cursed bad-temperedly.

Caught up in the atmosphere, it hadn't even occurred to Janine (who loved the smell and atmosphere a smoke machine created) to wonder who was operating it. They owned a smoke machine and sometimes at gigs even Janine's kids enjoyed operating it, crouched behind the Mistress backdrop behind the stage.

Nick and Fiona were on the lights. Riff's girlfriend was on the mixing desk. They had left the smoke machine at home. Jan felt the familiar knot creep into her stomach and her heart sank.

"Great gig, guys," the two 'Satisfaction' punters yelled as they lurched off, obviously satisfied.

"You should've played *Satisfaction,* though!"

Chapter Six

On the way home after the gig everyone was tired and sleepy, so Janine felt she didn't dare mention the smoke machine. Anyway, she was aware that her obsessive fears were getting on everyone's nerves. In truth, she felt that even mentioning the smoke machine would make her fears real again.

But the next day, after a Sunday morning hoover and tidy, she plucked up the courage to ring the pub.

Doing her utmost to sound nonchalant, she asked to speak to the manager and after an interminable wait of a few seconds he came to the phone. She thanked him for hosting the gig and said how great it had been. Then, oh so casually, added, "Would you pass on my thanks to whoever operated the smoke machine? That really added to the atmosphere." She was aware she sounded so falsely calm.

Then a silence hung in the air and the seconds seemed to last hours in her anxious anticipation.

"We presumed you'd brought it with you, love," the manager said distractedly – a little annoyed at being disturbed at such a busy time, Janine thought. She could hear the Sunday lunchtime banter in the background. "No idea who it was. Anyway, gotta go, sorry, love. Up to me eyes here."

And the phone went dead before she finished saying "OK, thanks. Sorry to bother you. B—"

At the next rehearsal the bass player did a 'no show' – and at the one after – so Janine took it on herself to ring him.

"I don't think we need to rehearse three times a week," he said.

"Well, the rest of the band thinks we do," Janine countered.

And that was that. Macho the other guys may have been, but it was Janine as usual who did the dirty work and fired him.

Fortunately Des knew of a bass player so he brought him to the next rehearsal. Janine just hoped he could play a solid 'bom bom bom' to form the backbone of the songs, rather than twiddly jazz style. And mercifully he did, at least to start with.

The band was rehearsing a new song about Knights of the Round Table. Janine wasn't a fanatic about the subject but she found it intriguing enough to write a song about. It came about from the germ of an idea – and a love of the fantastic name 'Lancelot'.

Lancelot

Oh my knight in armour
With wings and with your throne
Mount your white horse, mount your charger
All alone, all alone

Lancelot, deeds untold
Mysteries of your age unfold
Excalibur, mighty sword
Stronger than the Black Knight's word

Chorus
Lancelot, my knight in shining armour
Lancelot, Lancelot
Lancelot, my knight in shining armour
Lancelot, Lancelot

Lancelot, your quest is near
So in love with Guinevere
Serve the king but be aware
Keep your guard and say a prayer

Chorus

The song gave great scope for fun. Janine wrote the lyrics so that the last word of each verse could be wavered up and down as she sang them. And at a gig she could change Lancelot to 'wank a lot' just to see if anyone noticed.

The rehearsal passed without incident, much to Janine's relief. There were some moans about her singing out of tune and she longed for the time when they could get into a studio so she would be able to hear herself. How she envied those singers she watched on TV who appeared to hear even the slightest 'mmm' as they crooned along. All the talk was about paying for a studio session as the Mistress repertoire grew. Janine couldn't wait. She hoped that with all the new technology her voice would be enhanced and the band would agree she actually sounded great on tape. In the meantime, Des had spent even more money on little boxes of tricks that added echo to her voice.

It appeared the former bass player had also accused Janine of being 'too nice' to the audience, which was a bit 'uncool' for a rock singer. So she resolved to be a bastard to the audience at the next gig. Unfortunately the next gig was performing for a biker chapter of Hell's Angels. Hell.

Janine knew that she had to show no fear. It was in many respects like being a teacher having to deal with the toughest classes. Show any fear and they would make mincemeat of you. Being confident was all an act, but she was good at it – whatever she was feeling inside.

After fleeing for their lives at the end of the gig, mostly due to Janine calling the crowd 'a miserable bunch of bastards' when they didn't applaud, she was lambasted by the band for being too aggressive.

The bikers at least paid attention when Alex thrust his guitar backwards and forwards suggestively between Janine's legs.

Another couple of minor gigs followed, one in the upstairs bar of a really old pub in nearby Rugeley town – memorable for Des, bless 'im for his usual tact, asking the owner if they had rats. The rest of the band shifted uncomfortably and desperately tried to make light of the question.

The next gig was at a school hall a few miles away. Although it was a school, it boasted a proper concert hall with state of the art sound and lighting. Janine and Alex's neighbours Elaine and Mark turned up to show support. Elaine, being non musical, always joked that she would play the tambourine for them – but the beat was well and truly covered by wild Riff, crashing away on his kit like Animal from the Muppet Show.

After the gig Janine used the same loos as the audience and it was while she was in the loo that she overheard two girls talking about the band. 'Crap', was their considered opinion. 'Hey ho. Can't win 'em all,' Janine thought. She was so pleased with how the performance had been received overall that she wasn't going to let it bother her.

Back on home ground the next gig was in the huge function room at a local dog racing circuit and it was packed. Janine ignored the 'hi, Jan's all the way to the dressing room, desperately trying to stay focussed and keep the nerves in check. It felt like a walk to the executioner's chair. Martini Rosso in the dressing room again.

Also performing were Riff's favourite band, Dusty's Rusty Nuts and a Welsh band called Tredegar. The whole night was a triumph and everyone was on a high.

On nights like these, surrounded by rock fans, Janine savoured the atmosphere and thanked her lucky stars that she was living out her fantasy. It meant everything to her and tonight all the doubts, niggles and fears had disappeared. It was a gig that would be talked about for years – but not half so much as the next notorious performance.

Chapter Seven

Mistress was back in Lichfield for a 'Battle of the Bands' event. They hadn't entered the competition but had been invited to perform as part of the event's presentation night, so it was a no pressure gig.

The venue, called Enot's, was heaving. The band only had to perform a few songs. Everyone was there to have a good time, it was the end of the working week, the beer flowed and the atmosphere was one of fun.

The set opened with another guest band which featured stunning twin sisters as vocalists. Not only did they look great, they could actually sing. After their performance the 'battle' organiser, known as Titley, took to the stage to announce the winners and present trophies and medals.

"Wow!" he said, gesturing towards the twins. "Imagine if they had entered the competition!"

Janine wondered what Mistress would be like with three female lead singers. Now, what a band that would be!

Janine was bursting with pride when Titley called her kids up on stage. He presented them with a medal each for being brave enough to do the lights and smoke machine for Mistress's performance later. They looked genuinely flushed and chuffed and it was a sweet moment which she captured on video camera.

Next up for the presentation was Alan Greyman, young reporter for the local paper. Greyman had attended the 'battle of the bands' for weeks and had written his views in his 'Sounds' column. He was to be thanked for all the free publicity.

But Greyman had a pathological hatred of anything rock, preferring what he saw as the latest hip, modern sounds. It didn't matter how great a band was, if they played rock music they came in for Greyman's savage treatment. Janine was infuriated by most of his reviews. One particularly spiteful one was about one of her favourite bands. Adept with words he could savage a band intelligently and nastily.

So it was with some satisfaction that she witnessed the audience boo loudly as Greyman took to the stage.

Titley desperately tried to quell the noise, waving his hands up and down in front of him. "Wait till the big boys get hold of you," he told the bands in an effort to warn them the national press could be even worse.

During the interval Janine slid backstage to get changed, jostling with Riff for the one and only full-length mirror.

Janine had written lyrics for a new song, an absolute belter. It was fast-moving with a catchy, powerful chorus, bellowed out angrily by all the band members in unison as if they really meant it. They were going to play it for the first time in the set, always a nervous moment, but as usual it was well rehearsed. Janine wrote the lyrics after becoming increasingly frustrated with what she saw as universal apathy. It seemed to her that no-one got excited about anything. She remarked that if aliens landed the general public would just carry on watching *Coronation Street.* And so a song was born.

Don't Bother to Run

And they came out from the sky
People wondered why
Turned, shook their heads as they landed
No-one wanted to know
Turn over and watch the show
Sigh, it's all a bore
Can't take no more
Chorus
Don't bother to run
Don't bother to hide
Don't bother to run no more
Repeat

The *V* intro tape played menacingly, the crowd roared and the band blundered their way onto the stage in the darkness.

They romped through *Space is Ace, Run and Hide, XLR8, Lancelot* and *Don't Bother to Run.*

The new song went down such a storm that a mini stage invasion started. At one point there were so many audience members on the stage that it was difficult to see the band at all. But it was all light-hearted mayhem. Someone trod on a lead and it was yanked out of Des's guitar but the band played on until his sound was restored. Half a dozen guys surrounded Janine on the microphone, bellowing out the *Don't bother to Run* chorus. Others were stage diving into the audience.

Everyone was having a really great time – except Greyman. She spotted him, looking completely out of place in his ridiculous long overcoat, shirt and tie and shiny shoes, sidling off as inconspicuously as he could. He had seen enough. He was already concocting the first line of his review for next week's paper.

"Last week's Battle of the Bands presentation night proved to be an evening of torture—"

But for everyone else all was well with the world, all was good. Heads banged, fists punched the air. It was one of those special nights that would go down in history for those who attended.

Janine was in her element. Cue *Angel Rock* as the final song.

The crowd joined in, bellowing out the chorus:

> *And he packed his wings*
> *Took all his things*
> *Angel rockin' on high*

Janine did her usual thing: kneeling on the floor, lost in the moment, taking the chorus down low then building it up to its final crescendo with her eyes closed.

> *High high high*
> *(Like a mountain)*
> *High high high*
> *(Let me hear ya)*
> *High high high*

(I wanna hear ya).

She stood up slowly and opened her eyes for the final *high.*

Something was wrong; very, very wrong. But at first it didn't compute.

The audience's faces were level with hers. But these weren't the guys who had invaded the stage earlier.

'They've climbed on something', Janine thought, but there was something about their expressions that wasn't right. 'Bewilderment' was the word which came to mind – and a hint of fear in their eyes. It wasn't just a knot in her stomach this time; it was more like a meltdown.

She finished the final note and the band smashed into its sudden ending.

Janine darted a look at the rest of the band members but they seemed oblivious. They all had heads down, concentrating on the job at hand. But when they looked up, anticipating the cheers and ready to take their final bow they couldn't believe their eyes. The front three or four rows of people were – hovering – for want of a better word.

Instead of the usual cheer there were bewildered noises, a few screams and sounds of drunken bravado from some of the guys worse for wear.

One by one the front few rows descended slowly, back to the ground. It seemed that apart from a couple of guys at the back, who the band couldn't see in the darkness, the rest of the audience had not been affected – but they sure as hell saw what went on.

There was no encore when the lights went to blackout. People were talking animatedly, trying to make sense of what just happened and checking with everyone else, 'Did you see it? Did you see it?' 'Were you one of those that—that—levitated'?

Alex stormed up to Janine at the side of the stage. "What the fuck was THAT?" he asked her angrily and accusingly – as if she had engineered it.

"I don't know what the hell happened," she snapped back shakily. "But I've been trying to tell you for weeks there's something going on. Something isn't right."

"Well, you better come up with an explanation or we'll be a fucking laughing stock."

His words hurt, not just because he never usually even raised his voice, least of all swore at her, but because he clearly thought she had made it happen.

Titley was walking over to the band looking harassed and uptight. Alex pulled him over. "It's all right mate, just a new optical illusion we've been working on to add effect to the songs." Titley looked unconvinced. He had witnessed it himself.

Several crowd members came up to the band, asking what the hell happened. Riff made the most of the extra attention and thought only of the publicity this could gain. "Great illusion, innit? First time we've tried it. We'll see if we can pull it off again.

"It's Mistress magic," he added in a mock spooky voice. But for all his bravado he was one scared drummer.

Des and the bass player were huddled a little shakily at the side of the stage in quiet, intense conversation.

It took a while for the crowd to disperse. Titley stuck around until everyone was gone except for the band packing up the gear.

"Guys, we can't have this happening again," he said. "I don't know what you did but a lot of the punters were scared shitless. If this gets out I'll be ruined. Best keep it to yourselves."

The band members thought best of giving him any more 'optical illusion' bollocks so just agreed with him – then spent the rest of the night packing away quietly. They were so shell-shocked they didn't even discuss what had happened on the way home, didn't even say goodnight as they each got out of the van, each wondering where they would go from here.

Chapter Eight

The following day Janine was startled out of her thoughts when the phone rang. She actually jumped at the noise, with her nerves already in tatters. The last voice she expected to hear was the one at the end of the phone.

"Hello, is that Janine?"

A little hesitantly she answered, "Yes."

"Alan Greyman here, from the local paper's 'Sounds' column."

She bristled at his name.

"Yes?" she replied, a little too curtly perhaps.

Greyman went straight in for the kill.

"What's this I hear about your band making people think they'd levitated?"

"Dunno what you're talking about," she lied. "Obviously it's not possible."

Then she dropped the phone down on the receiver, almost as if the phone itself was contaminated with Greyman as long as she held the line open. She hadn't given him any information. There would be nothing for him to write. It would be a few days until the weekly paper came out anyway so she convinced herself it would be old news by Thursday.

She should have known better; it was front page news and the headline screamed at her.

Mistress Band Levitates Fans

by Alan Greyman

Fans of local rock band Mistress swear the music made them levitate three feet in the air at a gig in Lichfield on Friday.

Those at the front of the crowd claim they were left traumatised by the experience. Other fans say the ambitious band created an 'optical illusion' to further their career.

Lead singer Janine Lee was performing the closing number, Angel Rock, *singing the words, 'High, high, high' in the final chorus.*

Witnesses say the front rows lifted until their feet were level with the three-foot stage as they joined in the chorus.

A local psychiatrist, who does not wish to be named, said: 'Clearly this is a publicity stunt, an optical illusion or collective illusion brought on by hysteria'.

One fan who witnessed the event from the back of the hall added: 'What do you expect? The fans were probably high – high on drugs'.

Lead singer Janine denied any knowledge of the claims. 'Dunno what you're on about," she said. "Anyway, it's great publicity'.

Lichfield District Council chairman Councillor Dorothy Huff called on local venues to ban the band.

'We can't have this sort of thing in Lichfield,' she said. 'We are a proud tourist city which a reputation to uphold.

We cannot have a bunch of scruffy musicians sullying the good name of Lichfield'.

*Were you at the gig? Did you get 'high'? Let us know. Contact us on all the usual numbers.

Janine was raging. Greyman had even re-used the previous front page photo of her to go with the article. She flung the paper across the room. But her anger was fuelled by anxiety. She knew this would not go down well with her employers or band members.

She wasn't wrong. The next week released a torrent of rage, mostly from Alex.

"You're making us a laughing stock. You've got to stop this nonsense once and for all."

It didn't help when Riff's mates started yelling, 'Higher!' at him in the street or, 'Hey, it's Levitation Man!'

Des and the bass player escaped the worst of it as they lived out of the newspaper's circulation area.

At the next rehearsal session Janine got the impression that her days with the band were seriously numbered.

Before the first number she said, "Look. I know you don't believe me but I was not responsible for what happened."

"Nor the running man, nor the smoke, nor the fucking picture falling off the wall or the lights going out?" Des said. "Strange how it's always you talking about these things."

Janine felt tears welling up in her eyes but she didn't have the energy to retaliate. She loved these guys, they were her world. The band was due to rehearse a new song tonight so she hoped that would lighten the mood.

It was a fun, fast-paced song, based on a moment which occurred a few years ago when she went to see Alex's former band, called Earthquake. Janine had noticed a group of old ladies who were sitting in the Winking Frog pub before the band was due to perform. She thought how out of place they looked with all the denim and leather-clad youngsters around them and wondered whether they realised a wall of rock was about to hit them hard. She watched, amused, to see what their reaction would be when the band took to the stage.

The band ambled on in casual style and the old ladies took no notice. But the lead guitarist had only strummed a few chords to tune up when they threw their hands to their ears and took flight. Janine wasn't a bit surprised. But what did surprise her was that one of the old ladies stayed put. Not only did she listen to the first song, she sat and clapped at the end of it!

Janine never knew who the old dear was, but she thought she deserved a song of her own.

Old Lady Rock

Little old lady you sat there
With your long old coat and your greying hair
Surrounded by long hair and jeans
We expected you to leave.

The music was loud for your ageing ears
But you sat there and you clapped and you cheered
Although your friends all walked away
You decided to stay

Chorus
Old Lady Rock a song for you
You stayed, you sat and you heard us through
Old Lady Rock so out of place
With your orange juice and your wrinkled face

You didn't leave early just in case.
No

You sat alone through several songs
We could see it in your eyes it had been so long
The band played on, people stared
But you didn't care

Old Lady Rock now you're not alone
You got plenty of friends now to take you home
So put on your old grey mac
We expect to see you back

Chorus

The song sounded great in rehearsal so Janine felt a glimmer of hope.

The band then heard clapping. It was coming from someone standing in the doorway, a man, smart in an expensive suit.

'Please don't be paranormal', was all Janine could think, such was the extent of her paranoia nowadays.

But the very normal human being walked in and introduced himself.

"Hi. Miles Baxter, promoter. Someone sent me the article in your local newspaper so I thought I'd come and see you for myself. Took some tracking down to find out where you rehearse.

"You guys up for bigger things? We could use that article for publicity. Could be quite a lot of money in it for you. How do you fancy a stadium gig in Manchester? We'll get the story in the national press and we'll have no problem filling the stadium. You never know. It might encourage some more – er – 'air surfers', huh?"

"It wasn't true," Alex cut in. "Just something she thought up for publicity."

Janine glared at him and turned to Miles.

"Look, it did happen. I don't know how or why – but things happen when we play. I'm up for it, but this is out of our control. Maybe nothing will happen and everyone will be disappointed. But a stadium gig, with that many people? I have to tell you, I'm scared."

"Scared of performing to so many people?" Miles asked.

"No, scared of what'll happen," she said.

"We'll do it," Riff cut in. "This is what we've always wanted – to get the music out there."

And then Janine could hardly believe her ears. All the band members started back-tracking, ingratiating themselves with Miles, telling him how all these extraordinary things happened when they play, even inventing new 'happenings' to impress him.

A stadium gig and massive publicity was everything the band had hoped and worked for; but they had never seen it coming this way.

Chapter Nine

To perform a major indoor stadium gig was going to take some doing, but the band had a month to come up with a couple of new songs to pad out the set.

In the meantime the publicity machine went into overdrive. There were TV appearances, radio interviews, articles in magazines, posters with drawings of levitating fans with their arms held high. It was all quite surreal.

Janine seemed to be in a permanent state of anxiety and her fear rose to a new level. She had several main worries: that performing in front of a packed stadium nothing odd would happen, everyone would be disappointed and the band would be a laughing stock; that the band might not be up to a stadium performance and everyone would think they were rubbish; or something would happen with thousands of people witnessing it and she would have no control over what this would be.

It was decided that a professional lighting company would be used and that they should illuminate the stage in a simple, basic way. Nothing fancy, no tricks.

There would be a backdrop – a giant back cloth with the 'Mistress' logo in scary font across it and a support band to open the evening. There would be huge screens either side of the stage so the people at the back could see.

Careful consideration was given to the order of the songs so that ballads would be interspersed with more up tempo numbers. An instrumental number was also included which would give Janine a break from the vocals. While that was being performed she could grab a drink and just enjoy the moment on stage, moving to the music performed by 'her' talented guys.

The set list was decided:

Space is Ace
Old Lady Rock
Downhearted (new song)
XLR8
Underhand (new song)
Instrumental (no vocals)
Run and Hide
Don't Bother to Run
Lancelot
1984
Angel Rock

Assuming there was to be an encore it was decided to repeat *Don't Bother to Run*

There were also two 'standby' songs called *Vengeance* and *Hell's End* if needed, which had been written by Des.

Janine was pretty much angry about everything at the moment: at what she saw as a betrayal by the band (first blaming her then jumping on the bandwagon); at the spiteful headlines that were being churned out by Greyman in the local paper week in week out; at the bass player's sudden enthusiasm; and at being 'invited' to hand in her notice at work.

In a particularly despondent moment she did what she always did: wrote lyrics.

Oh you oughta crawl BACK under your stone
Lie FLAT, BENEATH. Make yourself at home!

Now, that outburst made her feel better.

She rehearsed constantly: at home, in the car, with the band, always conscious that she was the weakest member of the band and this was about to be exposed big time. She consoled herself that some of the biggest lead singers were not necessarily great vocalists, but they had a presence, or they were fun or inspirational. They had something.

With just a week to go before the gig, Greyman did his usual hatchet job on the front page.

Lichfield Band Brings City into Disrepute
by Alan Greyman

Local rock band Mistress look set to make our proud city a laughing stock when they perform a stadium gig next week.

The band, fronted by former local teacher Janine Lee, hit the headlines when their performances supposedly made their audience levitate. The claims, by inebriated fans, have since been de-bunked by professionals.

But worried local councillors fear 'the mud will stick' – and the city will be more famous for paranormal nonsense than for its history and magnificent cathedral.

Lichfield District Council chairman Councillor Mrs Dorothy Huff urged young people to boycott the Manchester stadium.

'I find it incredible that a band would stoop so low in order to gain publicity', Councillor Huff said. 'I sincerely hope young people channel their energy into more wholesome activities. We, the council, distance ourselves from the band. We deplore the effect this is having on our local music fans. 'Mistress' does not reflect the spirit and standing of our moral and upright city'.The leather clad lead singer and band members declined to comment.

Will you be attending the gig? Let us know on the usual contact numbers.

Of course the stadium gig was completely sold out – with coach loads of fans travelling from Lichfield.

Chapter Ten

All that was left to do was rehearse the two new songs.

The mood Janine was in made it easy to come up with lyrics for *Downhearted*.

Downhearted

And I'm in the pits
Looks like I've hit rock bottom
And I'm down the well
And I might as well
Stay hidden inside

Like a drowning man
With a gun in his hand
Futility
And I'm in the pits
Looks like I've hit rock bottom

Chorus

Clutchin' at a straw

Holdin' back the tide
Of the evil mind
I reach the point
Of no return
Looks like I'm gonna find
I'm
Downhearted
Downhearted
Downhearted
Downhearted

Janine loved the chorus in which the guys bellowed out the word, 'downhearted' and she repeated the word softly in the background, like an echo, at the end of each line.

New song *Underhand* was more down and dirty blues-y than the band had ever played before. Just playing on the word 'underhand' was ironic in itself, Janine thought as she rehearsed it. But she loved the laid back chorus, which she sang as if she was crying out the words.

Underhand

Chorus
Underhand, understand
Underhand, forever
Underhand, understand,
Underhand, forever

Adverts in the national press screamed out:
MISTRESS
ROCK BAND FAMED FOR LEVITATING ITS AUDIENCE

LIVE
MANCHESTER STADIUM
JUNE 26
EXPERIENCE AN UPLIFTING PERFORMANCE

No pressure then.

Promoter Miles didn't really care what happened at the stadium gig. He had sold every ticket and made shed loads of money. Mission accomplished. He never believed all that nonsense anyway, but he had enough about him to know how the publicity machine worked.

And this was how the band members looked at the gig too – except for Janine. But whatever happened (or not) was out of her hands now, she surmised.

Nerves would have gone into overdrive had the band not been so busy in the run-up to the performance. What with interviews, rehearsing and writing new songs the date was soon upon them, so it was a case of 'just do it'. And anyway, Janine had decided that instead of succumbing to nerves she would set her mind on performing as best as she could. After all, she believed in their songs and wanted to get their magic across to an audience.

Arriving at the stadium, Janine turned down the offer of her own dressing room. She found it oddly comforting to share a room with Riff. It gave some sense of normality, preening each other, adjusting tassels and messing with their hair. But this time they both had trembling hands.

They could hear the distant muffle of the support band. Janine knew Alex would be throwing up at this very moment, Des would be twiddling up and down the fret board at break-neck speed and the bass player – well, who knew what he would be thinking right now.

The call came from a technician for the band to begin the long walk through the corridors leading to the stage. They followed him as if they were going to their execution, only stopping briefly for Alex to heave up against a wall.

The support band had finished but the sound of the waiting crowd was deafening. They had started stamping on the ground in anticipation, thousands of feet creating a thunderous roar. There were whistles and sporadic chants moving round the hall like a Mexican wave.

Most were drunk – and they were ready to party.

Janine felt her legs shake and her teeth chatter with fright. She remembered the last time she felt like this was when she had to drive on her own for the first time, with no-one in that passenger seat. 'What an odd thing to think at this time', she laughed nervously at herself.

The *V* intro tape started. Oh, God—

The band members found their way to their positions on stage in the darkness and the expectation of the audience was palpable.

Janine stood with her back to the audience, palms sweating, the leather waistcoat sticking to her skin.

The roar of the helicopter effect came in, the lights came up – and BANG. The band launched into *Space is Ace*. What a rush. The affection from the crowd was almost a tangible thing and Janine resolved to enjoy this moment. Thousands of bright stars twinkled in the ceiling for the entire song, creating a magical atmosphere.

The band did the usual sudden ending – and never before had they felt such a rush of adrenaline as the crowd responded with a deafening, welcoming roar.

There were whistles directed at Janine as she walked across the stage, parading in her thigh-length boots and mini skirt. Now was the time to talk. She indicated for the audience to hush – and was amazed at how powerful it felt when they did.

Standing in the darkness, with just a spotlight on her, Janine looked tiny and vulnerable in the vast auditorium. But she spoke clearly and projected her voice with determination.

"Hello, Manchester! (Laughing) That's a cliché I know, but I've always wanted to say that! (Cheers from the crowd).

"This is just awesome." (The band looked a bit uncomfortable, not expecting this early interruption to the performance and wondering what the hell she might say. After all, she'd never quite got it right even at small time gigs – too nice, too aggressive, they remembered).

"You've all read the publicity. I honestly don't know what's going on – or whether we'll experience anything or not. I don't know what's created by lighting effects or what isn't any more." She glanced to the ceiling and felt unnerved to realise there were no bulbs which could have created the starry effect – but perhaps they were projected.

"I just want everyone to be safe," she continued sincerely. "Enjoy the gig. If nothing happens, that's out of my control. If anything does happen – well, we'll share it together."

There was a huge applause and she resolved there would be no more interruptions. In rock star mode, she indicated to the band to launch into the rest of the set.

"*Old Lady Rock*!" (Roar from the audience, their hands held high).

They were loving it. It was a perfect song to keep the momentum going.

At the end of the second verse Janine looked up – and she saw her – right there on the front row: an old lady, wearing a grey mac. How out of place she looked, clapping sweetly, squeezed in by burly guys.

The crowd saw her too. Her petite frame was shown on the giant screens, which emphasised her wrinkles. Janine feared the poor dear would be squashed and darted her eyes at security. But when she glanced back the old woman was gone. Janine just prayed she wasn't being trampled underfoot.

Next up: *Downhearted*. And the band was relieved to get through the song without any mistakes. Janine was relieved to get through the song without incident.

"This next song is called *XLR8*!" Janine, confident now, announced.

All of the band's lyrics had been printed in nationwide publicity articles so the crowd bellowed out every single word in glorious unison. They seemed to get it – changing '*XLR8*' subtly to the word 'accelerate'. Janine was impressed and did the posing thing of holding out the microphone for the audience to take over the vocals.

And the running man was back – careering around the wall of the entire auditorium. The crowd showed their appreciation with a roar of approval. This is what they had read about, and whether it was lighting effects or not, they didn't really care. The man's shape, a brilliant white, shot around the top of the wall, taking just seconds to complete a sweep of the whole stadium. The effect was almost strobe-like for the rest of the song. Janine had a bad feeling about this but at the same time felt almost defiant. 'I'm gonna do this gig and we're performing right to the end, whatever happens', she thought. She became almost steely-eyed, such was her determination.

Next up – *Underhand*, which Janine introduced as a new song and she really enjoyed gyrating centre stage in time with the rhythmic, laid back, blues-y beat – at times with her back to the audience, facing Riff, and conducting the band as if certain parts of the song were synchronised to her movements, with the drop of an arm or the punch of a fist into the air.

The instrumental came next, a chance for Janine to snatch a drink off stage, sidle back on then adopt various air guitar poses with Alex and Des. Thanks to the band's accomplished musicianship the instrumental piece went down a storm, particularly Riff's crashing drum solo in the middle.

'So far so good', Janine thought.

She glanced at the set list to remind her which song came next. *Run and Hide.* She was almost about to introduce the song with a tantalising mock scary voice when Alex started improvising. Furious with him deviating from the super-rehearsed set, she darted a look at him hoping to catch his eye. But he was really into his creepy introduction to the next song – and with a shiver, Janine realised it was the same piece that he had played that night when the picture fell down. She did an arms outstretched pose which looked fittingly menacing, but inside she was fuming, scared that he was tempting fate. The funereal sound echoed around the stadium and the spotlight settled on Alex, playing as if transfixed.

The hall was plunged into darkness. Not normal darkness, but a blackness you could not imagine. Not even the exit signs were lit up. There was an audible gasp from the audience caught up in the atmosphere. One very dim light slowly hovered above Alex as he played – and almost instinctively Janine thought the only way to break the 'spell' was to announce in her best creepy voice, "Ladies and gentlemen. *Run and Hide.*"

Believing it was all part of the show. the audience gave a slightly nervous cheer.

Janine's plan worked. Alex seemed to snap out of his trance and the power chord introduction (still creepy, but not as creepy as his improvisation) echoed around the auditorium – which remained in pitch darkness.

Janine took centre stage and directed the song straight at the audience.

Did you watch the late night show?
Are you walkin' home alone?
Hearin' footsteps just behind
Horror stories now crowd your mind

Shapes on your bedroom wall
Look behind you – and that ain't all
Fear the night it's so cold
Icy fingers around your soul.

And did it really go that icy cold? Just a minute ago the band were sweating under the stage lights. How could it possibly be this cold? The cold and dark were almost tangible and every word of the song seemed to hit home.

The words *run and hide* in the chorus seemed to take on renewed significance. That's exactly what the band and the audience felt like doing. And they weren't exactly singing along with this one.

Icy fingers around your soul indeed.

In truth, Janine was glad when the song was over and the lights returned to normal. The applause was genuine, but there was a change in the crowd as they wondered, just like Janine, which parts were showmanship and which were unplanned.

'The promoter could have arranged for all this to happen', Janine reassured herself. 'It's in his financial interest if the band gets more publicity'.

Cue Janine's best amateur dramatic skills.

Acting as if there was no problem at all and that last fiasco was all planned, she announced cheerfully, "Hey, I can see ya. Warming up now?

Encouraged by her confidence, there was a resounding cheer.

"*Angel Rock*!" somebody yelled from the back of the auditorium.

"Later," she replied in mock scary voice. "Next up we have a song about people not giving a shit. Do you give a shit?"

"No!" came the reply from hordes of adrenalin-fuelled fans.

So Janine seized the momentum.

"Do you give a shit? I didn't quite hear ya."

"No!" (Louder.)

"Can't hear ya. Do you give a shit?"

"No!" they screamed at the top of their lungs.

"Don't Bother to Run!"

And the band burst into *Don't Bother to Run*.

This was a gift of a chorus for a sing-a-long together. The mood lightened and everyone leapt up and down so much during the chorus that Janine wondered if the floor would cave in. She could actually feel the thunderous roar of all those feet pounding on the ground together.

Janine signalled to the band to quieten down for one of the choruses, which she sang really low. Then, indicating with her arms, the band broke the sound barrier for the final chorus – just as spaceship lights appeared where the running man had once fled around the hall. It was a complete ring of lights filling the roof of the auditorium.

And even though the band was playing at full volume, the surreal sound of the spaceship was deafening – so much so that the crowd had their hands to their ears. And a sudden downward blast of air shook the crowd so much that they visibly jostled to keep their footing. And on the last note of the song, perfectly timed – poof – it was gone.

Janine gave up all pretence of confidence.

"Fuck! Everyone OK?"

And a muted response, intermingled with false bravado cheers, came back to her. They knew, and she knew, there was no technology at the time which would pull that off.

"Do you want some more?" Janine said, rather than shouted rock-star style.

Roar from the crowd.

She took a moment to look at the other band members. Alex looked ready to throw up. Des looked completely nonplussed, as if he had no idea what the hell was going on. Riff was all bravado – standing on his drum stool and hyping up the crowd – and the bass player was preparing for some major strutting.

"OK, here we go. *Lancelot.*"

Heavy on power chords and vocals, the rock ballad sounded brilliant. And in true Mistress style there was a catchy, simple chorus which just begged for the audience to join in.

Lancelot
My knight in shining armour
Lancelot, Lancelot.

The two side screens were filled to capacity with the most beautiful white horse, complete with knight in shining armour and the crowd roared their approval.

'Now, that's impressive', Janine thought. 'But I thought the screens were just supposed to show the band and the audience'.

Janine actually turned sideways on to watch the screens for herself. It also gave her the opportunity to visit both sides of the stage and direct her singing to different areas.

The audience was transfixed by the absolute beauty of the images as the horse reared and pranced his way gracefully through the song. It was a truly awesome scene, which faded out on the last line of the song.

The applause was deafening – more for the horse than Janine's singing.

"*Angel Rock!*" came the call again.

Janine was now actually feeling exhausted and the band members looked absolutely knackered. After all, this was their first ever stadium gig. Despite their tight rehearsals, they hadn't realised the sheer relentlessness of powering through one song after another – and having to really put on an act at the same time. Janine took time to grab a bottle of water (no Martini for this gig, all concentration required) from the side of the stage during the applause. The swig felt glorious and she began to look forward to the ordeal being over.

She decided honesty was the best policy.

"How you doin'?" she addressed the crowd (mock rock voice back).

Roar from the crowd.

"Dunno about you, but I'm shattered. You want some more?"

Roar from the crowd.

She paused for a few moments to allow the guys to get themselves together and mop themselves up with towels. During the pause she could feel the electricity of anticipation and felt that familiar knot of fear return. But the next song was harmless.

"1984."
(Cheers)
Silver trail lined with gold
There's a tale that I've been told
Followin' a yellow brick road
In no man's land
In no man's land
In no man's land

The tune was quite cheerful. Not even the golden rain falling from the ceiling could dampen the atmosphere.

"Rain? What rain? We're indoors," Janine almost screamed to herself.

Fine, golden particles rained down on the crowd. They jumped up to catch them and threw bundles of misty rain back into the air. Even the tough macho guys were laughing at the feelgood factor. As soon as the rain hit the ground it disappeared, just as a bubble pops in the air. It looked just magical. And through the rain, stretching across the auditorium was the most beautiful rainbow, which actually brought gasps from the crowd as it slowly appeared then vanished after a couple of minutes.

Janine felt breathless. Paranormal or not, it really was the most beautiful sight she had ever seen.

"Wow!" she said into the mike. "How amazing was that?"

Roar from the crowd.

She paced up and down, backwards and forward across the stage, taking time to prepare for the finale, keeping the audience waiting. The reason was twofold: so she could breathe deeply to calm her nerves; and because she did the rock star thing of deliberately heightening the audience's anticipation.

"*Angel Rock*!" came the cry again – and slowly a chant developed around the hall as she paced and breathed deeply.

"*Angel Rock! Angel Rock! Angel Rock!*"

She knew perfectly well the song's reputation had preceded it.

After a deep breath Janine announced: "Manchester, you have been brilliant. *Angel Rock*!"

The opening bars of the song rang out and were received by the biggest cheer of the night. Janine felt as if the wall of emotion emanating from the crowd was enough to knock her backwards.

There was an angel knew him well
Went to heaven but found it hell.

The crowd was really with her, singing their hearts out, but when it came to the chorus the energy was taken to a completely new level.

So he packed his wings

Took all his things
Angel rockin' on high

Janine felt that if she never did anything else with her life it wouldn't matter. This moment was enough. This feeling was the one she had hankered for ever since experiencing the buzz of watching her first rock band live. Now she too knew how it felt.

The song passed by, oh so quickly and soon the gig would end. Janine was on the floor, gyrating suggestively for the last lines of the song. Into quiet mode, slowly rising, arms ready to punch the air for the final note.

High high high
Like a mountain
High high high
I wanna hear ya
High high high

And there they were – euphoric. Thousands of fans, singing their hearts out – with expressions that were a mixture of wonder and abject fear. Many had their arms outstretched, some held their fists in the air. And almost every audience member was hovering about three feet from the ground, legs and feet calm and still. There were more guys than girls in the audience. A few girls' screams could be heard around the stadium but most people, caught up in the moment of a lifetime, were enjoying the phenomenon. Janine continued to sing softly. The band was waiting for her signal for the sudden ending, but she walked backwards and forwards across the stage, arms outstretched to the audience, taking in a sight which no person in the world had ever seen before.

High high high
High high high

And then the music died. The power had been cut off completely and the auditorium was surrounded by burly security guys in uniform. The magic was broken and there was to be no encore. Janine watched, entranced, as slowly, one by one, her audience glided down onto firm ground.

The police were on stage and a loud hailer announcement was made that everyone was to leave the stadium in a quiet, orderly way – now. The security men would ensure no one rushed and they were to go home quietly, they were told.

In no uncertain terms the band was ordered to get off the stage, but just before she did so Janine kissed her hands and 'threw' the kisses to every corner of the auditorium. The audience, as one, threw one back. She waved and shouted a 'thank you' – but without a microphone, her tiny voice was lost in the vast open space. Then she was roughly manhandled off the stage.

Chapter Eleven

The Health and Safety people went crazy.

The fans, gathered outside the auditorium, talked long into the night about their experience and it took the police well into the early hours to move them. Even then, it was only after a bus load of fans was arrested, that others reluctantly agreed to move on.

Janine and the band were forced into a waiting police van and taken off for questioning. The promoter was brought in to give his account of the evening and he confirmed he had made no arrangement whatsoever for any special effects. He was as astounded as everyone else.

But the police were in no mood to talk about the wonder of it all. Janine had a policeman's face just inches from hers bellowing accusations and words like 'irresponsible' at her.

"Do you have NO regard for the safety of your fans?

"You do know you're finished, don't you?

"We will make sure this band never takes to the stage anywhere in the country again.

"Do you realise the cost of having to use hundreds of police tonight?

"What makes you think you can go around putting people's lives at risk?

"What if someone had fallen?

"WHAT THE HELL DO YOU THINK YOU WERE DOING?"

And on it went, throughout the night.

Protestations fell on deaf ears. The rest of the band, including Alex, blamed Janine for 'inciting' the fans. They were all eventually released, exhausted, without any official charges, but with a severe ticking off and a warning that they had not heard the last of this.

The national press had a field day. Scores of fans came forward, all giving similar testimonies.

Janine contacted the venue, still concerned about the fate of the old lady, convinced she would be told some old dear had been found trampled underfoot. But there were no such reports. In fact there had been no injuries during the entire evening.

The doubters also had a field day. There was a flood of articles in national magazines and newspapers from 'experts' in various fields. Every one rubbished the fans' stories. It was mass hysteria, hypnotism, clever illusions or some bizarre collective lie being used to drum up more publicity for the band.

But the policeman's threat turned out to be true. Due to health and safety fears, no venue in the land would book Mistress.

Greyman was in his element on the front page.

Lichfield Band Come Home in Disgrace
by Alan Greyman

Local rock band Mistress is finished.

Promoters have seen through the band's bizarre attempts at self publicity and a police health and safety warning has been issued.

Mistress is banned from appearing at venues across the country.

Lichfield District Council chairman Councillor Dorothy Huff said she was 'delighted' by the news.

'I am pleased this nonsense ends here,' she said. 'This band has been an embarrassment to the city. I hope they all now smarten themselves up and go out and get proper jobs.'

Lead singer Janine Lee has hardly ventured out of her home since the Manchester debacle and rumour has it she is planning to leave the city.

She declined to make any comment.

Ms Lee has been accused of corrupting the minds of young people by encouraging them to believe they were taking part in paranormal activity. Experts have ridiculed her claims that almost an entire auditorium levitated in response to the band's music.

Editor's note: as a responsible local paper we urge young people to engage themselves in more wholesome activities in the future.

Janine consoled herself by putting the article face up in the cat's litter tray. She scattered the litter, imagining with some satisfaction what would land on the name Greyman.

The kids were with their dad for the weekend and Alex was out drowning his sorrows with Riff somewhere. She wondered how on earth the band was going to survive this. They had all come so far together and had so much more to give. Despite everything, surely now was the best time to go into the studio and record.

The phone rang and she cautiously answered, relieved that it was Des.

"Hi," he said quietly. "We've all had a chat and we've decided it's best if we end it here. Me and the bass player have been writing songs and we think we can do OK. Riff thinks the songs are good. We can still play some Mistress songs under our new name as I co-wrote some of them.

"I've spent lots of money trying to make you sound good, but it's not been enough. You look great, but the vocals just aren't there – and, well, whatever's been going on, is down to you, we think.

"We've asked the twin girls to front our new band. Don't know what Alex will do. That'll have to be up to him to decide."

Feeling as if she had been knifed in the heart several times by Des's quiet words, Janine simply said, "OK. Thanks for being honest with me."

But a part of her had died – even before she put the phone down.

Alex had already suggested bringing the twins into the band to strengthen the vocals and Janine would have had no problem with that. But the thought of them singing Mistress songs without her was too much to bear. She had no idea what Alex would decide to do and she didn't want to influence him either way.

Not sure what to do with herself, Janine did what she did best. She took out a pen and paper and wrote a letter to Alex; not a pleading one, but one that told him how she felt and that she would be heartbroken if the band continued with the name Mistress without her, singing her songs. She told him if he wished to continue with the other guys without her she understood.

Another massive hurdle weighed heavily on her mind. Even if Alex stayed with her, the thought of starting over again, just the two of them, was so daunting – emotionally and financially. Des would want his equipment back and there would be that whole process of auditioning all over again. There would have to be a new name, a new identity. And anyway, who would dare form a band with the mistress of magic?

She left the note on the kitchen table and, still not knowing how to ease the pain, Janine left the house, got into the car and drove off into the dark, rainy night with nowhere in particular to go.

She had only driven to the top of the road when the tears started to flow. It was as if the tears mirrored the rain pouring down the windscreen. Just as the windscreen wipers tried their best to clear the screen, so she blinked furiously, determined not to cry.

This was more than just a band. This was her life – one that she had relished every moment of. The tears came relentlessly, so much that it was getting difficult to drive.

It was a dark, winter night and the headlights coming from the opposite direction were blinding as she desperately tried to stop the tears. She felt she had no choice but to pull over at the next layby which happened to be outside the village post office. At least no-one would see her here, crying so hard that she thought her heart would break; crying so much that the sound of the sobs seemed to come from afar and made her feel sorry for herself. She couldn't remember ever crying so hard in all her life. And sitting looking at the post office made her feel ridiculous. 'What a stupid place to drive to, you're pathetic', was all she could think.

Janine scrabbled around in the car for some tissues to wipe her nose and face and still the tears overflowed, unstoppable. She sat there for about an hour, feeling the saddest it was possible to be. Looking in the rear view mirror she could see that she looked a complete sight.

There was a little part of her that had to acknowledge some of the tears were of relief. There would be no more stage fright, no more arguments, no more worrying about singing in key.

But there were the hottest, burning tears for the 'what ifs?'.

What if they had gone into the recording studio – and with all that technology they could have sounded great?

What if a whole new audience could have heard those songs and loved them just as much as she did?

Exhaustion was the only thing that eventually stopped the tears. Janine sat in the darkness, the lights of passing cars flashing by, and just stared ahead.

'What about Alex?' she thought. Would he still want to carry on without her? Or would he want to start a new band with her?

Janine started up the car and drove back home, feeling like an empty shell. Alex was already in the doorway looking frantic.

"Where have you been? I've been ringing everyone. I thought – when I read the letter—"

"Just been driving," she replied. "Don't worry, I wasn't going to kill myself," she said dryly – aware of what a sight she looked.

They talked long into the night. Alex had already decided he had had enough. He had been in bands long before Mistress and actually he was glad of the split. He was sick of all the arguments, the hard work – and especially the latest stress.

A few days later Des collected his equipment but it was more than Janine could bear to watch him take it. She stayed in the bedroom while Alex talked pleasantries, made embarrassed apologies and helped him load the gear into a van. Janine blamed Des for the split, however politely he had broken it to her. He and the bass player could have backed her, but decided to go their own way writing Beatles-type songs.

She was also disappointed in Riff. He could have chosen to stay, which would have made it less daunting to start up a new band. But he chose to join Des and the bass player – for the time being anyway. Where to go from here?

Chapter Twelve

For weeks Janine could not bear to even listen to tapes of Mistress music – in fact any music. It was as if the very life had been sucked out of her. Music was so important in her life, but now it only served to make her cry. Any record that she listened to, including those which were her absolute favourites, simply reduced her to tears. The words all seemed to have double meanings and she found it unbearable to listen to any bands at home, in the car, anywhere.

She and Alex were still remarkably besotted and did their best to get by as a couple, an ordinary couple, as opposed to two band members. And she was relieved that they were still in love. She had often wondered whether they would survive without the common interest of the band. Alex continued to work and was happy to lead a quieter life; Janine found a part time teaching job at a college in a neighbouring town where she was less well known.

Janine had always been the party animal, the one to instigate a night out somewhere. But now, without her precious band, she had no desire whatsoever to go anywhere to rock out. To watch a local band play was too painful, just a reminder of what she had lost and only stirred an urge within her to get back on that stage. She was so desperately sad about Mistress, but too despondent to start over again. As a born freedom fighter, she knew that this was not her usual character. And somewhere, deep within her soul she had a feeling that the extraordinary events of the last few months could surely not have been for nothing.

In the meantime, the only thing that came close to giving her any peace of mind was to sit somewhere picturesque, reading a book. She could lose herself in a biography or well-written novel, entranced by someone else's trials and tribulations. But even this was flawed since the weather was usually grey, drizzly or freezing, which left her moping about the house almost screaming with frustration at how ordinary everything seemed. She wondered why she could not settle for this. After all, this was how most people spent their lives, wasn't it?

The sun came out at last for one glorious day. With Alex at work and the kids at school, Janine decided to take herself off to Lichfield, find a nice spot by the Arts Centre next to the pool and sit with a book and a drink. Perhaps she could find some solace sitting in the sunshine, watching the swans glide by and enjoying the view of the cathedral's three spires.

But everything annoyed her.

A child was screaming and misbehaving – and the mother did nothing to correct the little monster. A car screeched round the corner with rap music blaring, the bass thumping out of the open windows for all to hear. 'Obviously the inconsiderate twat has a small penis', Janine thought to herself. A persistent bee just would not get the message and fuck off away from her can of diet Coke, no matter how often Janine took a swipe at it.

And it was hot, too hot in the midday sun.

Janine may now be a former rock star, but she still could not bring herself to wear anything remotely conventional and 'dressing for comfort' was not in her vocabulary. Today, on one of the hottest days of the year so far, she was wearing tight blue jeans, a black sleeveless T shirt with a simple guitar motif on it, her trademark black fringed boots with heels (boots, for goodness sake, on a summer's day), socks inside the boots (what, on a day like this?) and sunglasses perched on top of her head – like a hair band holding back the flowing locks. She liked clothes that were black or blue, plain but pretty, but with a hint of 'rock'. Most women were out and about in their floral frocks and sandals today – a look that Janine felt a pathological hatred for; one that she would often decry with the phrase 'I wouldn't be seen dead in that'. 'And what a stupid expression is that?' Janine thought, her mind wandering as usual. 'How would you have much choice if you were dead anyway'?

But today, the black T shirt only served to attract the sun. Even her black, fringed shoulder bag felt hot and she felt slightly ridiculous wearing boots.

Conversely, in the winter she would never wear enough. Ever protective, Alex would insist, 'Put your coat on, wear your gloves, do your coat up, put a jumper on', all of which fell on deaf ears.

'We are never satisfied, are we'? Janine thought. 'We moan when it rains, we moan when it's hot'.

Her eyes were so sensitive to the sun that it almost hurt to look at the white pages. Exasperated, she snapped the book shut, put it in her bag, wore her sunglasses properly and scanned the area desperately for somewhere shady to sit.

The cathedral clock rang out for twelve noon.

'That's it,' she thought to herself. 'It's been ages since I visited the cathedral. It'll be cool and peaceful in there. I might as well have a look around while I'm here.'

Janine made her way along the winding pathway to the magnificent Cathedral Close, feeling hotter and more uncomfortable with every step. But she smiled to herself at her audacity of walking into a cathedral after writing a song like *Angel Rock*. She just hoped if there was a God that He or She or Whatever had a sense of humour.

Walking into the medieval cathedral Janine was immediately struck by how dark and cool the interior was. And it was so quiet, blissful. All that could be heard was the faint clack of heels on the cold hard floor. There were just a few visitors that day. Janine watched them as they stopped to admire the architecture, lit candles and talked in whispers. As someone who was not remotely interested in historic buildings she felt a bit of a fraud in the cathedral's magnificent interior. And she felt slightly guilty that people came from abroad to admire this magnificent cathedral, yet as a local she had only been there twice before.

'I'll bring the kids here', she thought. 'They really should see what's on their doorstep'.

She spent about an hour wandering around the nooks and crannies, reading the information provided and sat for a while on one of the benches just staring ahead, saying a private prayer, asking for peace of mind or for her life back – but not feeling anything in return.

'Ah well, it was cool and quiet', she thought to herself and got up to leave.

As she turned to walk back out through the main doors, the sun streamed through one of the painted glass windows, lighting up a concentrated area of the aisle in front of her. The sight in front of her took her breath away. Standing a few feet ahead, in the sun's rays, was the most beautiful young man she had ever seen in her entire life – so perfect that she was convinced he must be a vision. Entranced, she stood to take in what was surely an answer to her prayers. Bathed in sunlight, he had long blond hair and was wearing a flowing white shirt which hung over tight, light-blue jeans. His white trainers only served to add to the spectacle. The whiteness of his shirt reflected the strong sunbeam back at her too-sensitive eyes. She tried to use her hands to shade the sunlight so she could make sense of what stood before her.

"Janine?" he said.

Startled that this extraordinary being had spoken to her, Janine just stood open-mouthed and was aware that she was shaking slightly – not so much that anyone else would notice, but enough that she was aware. She moved towards him and he stepped sideways out of the sun's rays. But my God, lit up or not, he was still the most perfect human being she had ever seen in her life.

Perhaps mistaking the effect he had on her, he attempted to apologise.

"Sorry, I just wanted to check it was you. I didn't mean to startle you."

"You know me?" was all she could think of to say, and the words came out a bit croaky, she thought. She felt her heart thumping as they continued to walk towards the exit, still not sure if he was real or not.

They passed through an area that was quite dark and gloomy on their way out, but even in the half light, the sight of this young man still took her breath away. She wanted to take in every aspect of his appearance. He had the smoothest and most flawless skin; clean-shaven, he looked younger than she supposed, perhaps in his early thirties; and he had an air of confidence – as if he knew how beautiful he was. His hair was blond, tumbling down his back and over his shoulders, clean and slightly wavy. And he wore a simple silver bracelet on his left arm (plain but pretty) with two diamonds encased in it. He smiled at her, as if to give reassurance, and the skin around his piercing blue eyes crinkled ever so slightly. Janine's heart leapt. How was it possible to look even more gorgeous?

"I'm sorry, I didn't mean to stalk you or anything," he said. "I saw you walking away from the pool but I wasn't sure if it was you in those big sunglasses. So I thought I'd wait around and pluck up the courage to ask you. So, here I am," he added, twiddling his bracelet around.

'What could this amazing creature POSSIBLY want with me'? was all Janine could think.

But they were now walking side by side back towards the pool. And even being next to him was like a re-awakening. At thirty years old she felt proud to be even associated with this guy, even though she had met him just a minute or two ago; and she wondered whether passers-by would think they were a couple. He was taller than her (well, most people were) but he was of average height. She knew nothing about him, but she already knew they looked great together – and she had never felt anything like this in her life.

"I'm in a rock band," he said matter-of-factly.

'Could this get any better'? Janine thought.

"I was at your gigs at Enot's and Manchester with the guys and we all thought the shows were amazing. We've been trying to get hold of you now all that stuff's died down. We wondered if you wanted to join our band? I'm the lead singer."

'Could this REALLY get any better'?

And he went on; babbling a bit nervously now, Janine thought, but even that was endearing.

"We have two gorgeous backing girl singers – actually they're twins – and we really want to go places. We thought it you would agree to join us, sharing front vocals with me, what a great band that would be, something different. And you should be back on stage. It's like you've gone underground. No-one's heard of you since—"

Janine was aware that she had hardly spoken a word yet. She wanted to say something that was an intelligent response, something that would impress him, but all that tumbled out of her mouth slowly and accidentally was, "You-are-so-beautiful."

And he laughed – which made her laugh.

"What's your name?" she asked.

"Dion," he said softly.

Dion. She said it over and over to herself in her head, reminding herself of the scene in the musical *West Side Story* when lead character Tony can't stop saying the name of the girl he just met, Maria, because it sounded so wonderful.

"What's your band called?" she said, distracted by his perfect white teeth.

"Son of Gabriel," he replied, with a knowing glint in those steely blue eyes.

"Of course," was all Janine could say.

Chapter Thirteen

Dion and Janine, Dion and Janine, Dion and Janine.

Even just saying the words made her feel as if she had already betrayed Alex.

After sitting on a bench near Minster Pool in Lichfield, she had walked with Dion to the car park near to the Arts Centre and waved him off as he put on his shades to shield those beautiful eyes from the sunshine. He drove off in his blue TVR sports car. 'What else would he drive'? Janine thought to herself.

They had talked about the Mistress phenomenon and his words lingered in her head as he drove away.

"There's something special that happens when an audience is really with you," he had said. "I felt it that day in the stadium. It's a strange feeling, one that I've experienced myself as a performer and as someone in an audience.

"For a couple of hours it's as if you and the audience are one – all under one roof, all – all connected by something. It's the music, yes, but it's something more than that—"

He had laughed at himself, talking in such deep terms with someone he had just met.

"God, what do I sound like?" he'd asked with an apologetic smile. "But I think you know what I mean. It's also something to do with you – and when you get the right people around you. That's when something happens. I would love it if we could recreate some of that stuff with our music."

She had never been able to speak on such a spiritual level with any other human being, male or female, in her entire life.

One thing had puzzled her. If he had been at the Enot's gig she was sure she would have noticed him standing out like a beacon, but she could not very well say that.

"I don't remember seeing you at the Enot's gig," she said, trying to sound casual.

"I came in late. I'd been to the Bowling Green pub for my boss's fortieth birthday, but I left the party early so I could catch at least some of your gig with my mate Tommy. Anyway, it was packed when we got there so we stood right at the back and managed to catch the last couple of songs. We were among those who were – erm – affected."

He was running his fingers through his hair to keep it from falling into his eyes.

And she replayed over and over the way he asked her, "Will you come to our band rehearsal next Sunday?" and how his eyes looked into hers as if his life had depended on her answer.

She knew she was already besotted. Her stomach lurched at the thought of seeing him again. This was love at first sight. It did exist after all; but how cruel. How could it be possible to fall for someone when you were already deeply in love with someone else? It wasn't even as if she was looking elsewhere.

Dion hadn't mentioned a girlfriend and she had been too scared to ask him. He mentioned Alex as the rhythm guitarist's name in Mistress and said how impressed he had been with him as a performer and song writer. There had been so much stuff about Mistress in the press, he was obviously aware that Janine and Alex were an item, but to her shame she hadn't mentioned him at all.

He had been in various bands for years, he told her, but he felt everything had come together with Son of Gabriel.

How to get through the next four days until the rehearsal? And what to tell Alex? When she got home about four o'clock Alex's van was already parked outside the flat. 'Home early', she thought and tried to put on a normal face and say a cheerful/normal 'hi' as she walked into the lounge.

"All right?" he asked, without looking up from the telly. "Good day?"

'I'll just blurt it out and get it over with straight away', Janine thought.

"Had a really good day. I went to Lichfield because it was too nice to stay in. And you'll never guess what? There was this guy who noticed me from the band and he came over to talk to me. Turns out he's in a band and wants me to go to a rehearsal with them on Sunday. What do you think?"

"Yea – if you want," he said, adjusting the volume upwards on the remote control.

"He seems really nice," Janine tried again.

"Good. Go for it if you want to."

'You have no idea what you are saying', she thought to herself and went to the bedroom to check her make-up and hair in the mirror. There was a little smear of mascara under her eyes. She hoped Dion hadn't noticed. She turned sideways, as she often did, to check her weight. Tummy tucked in, not looking too bad. Then she took a really hard look at herself. 'You could back out now. You know perfectly well where this is going', she said to herself in the mirror.

Over dinner Alex had asked half-heartedly what the band's name was.

"Son of Gabriel," she replied.

He snorted a laugh. "Not very rock and roll, is it?" he said.

"It is a rock band," Janine told him but was unable to meet his gaze. "I'd heard of them anyway. They've been on the local scene for a couple of years. They've already got two girl backing singers, but want to try me on vocals with the front man. Why don't you come along and see what you think?" The invitation to Alex was an attempt at saving herself, from herself.

"Promised to help Nick sort out his car on Sunday," was the response that sealed the final nail in the coffin.

That night in bed they were back to their usual amorous selves. But snuggled in her favourite position, sleeping curled around his back, Janine's thoughts were elsewhere.

Since the band had split up Janine still had not sung a single note. She did not even listen to music on the car radio. The old Janine would have sung her heart out to all the rock classics – even imitating the lead guitar riffs which she knew note-perfect. But the new, broken Janine felt she had little to sing about.

But with in effect an audition taking place on Sunday, she thought she had better fill the next few days with some serious vocal stretches. She couldn't bring herself to sing Mistress songs but instead sang along to AC/DC, Queen, Iron Maiden, Journey – finding the range and trying to project her voice. And some of that old self began to emerge and there was a little fluttering of something inside of her.

'It feels as if this was meant to be', she told herself. 'But what if I'm wrong? What if I make a complete tit of myself'?

Work and the kids kept her busy for the rest of the week. And she was going out for a meal with Alex on Saturday night. That would pass the time until Sunday. It was their favourite Indian restaurant and Alex had booked a small, private booth so they could enjoy their meal in peace without Janine moaning about noisy customers. This was typical of her character – a contradiction in many respects. Love loud music, hate other people's loud chatter; love hanging out drinking with the lads, but equally love a challenging, intellectual play or movie; not keen on children, adored her own kids.

Alex looked handsome tonight, she thought. He had spruced himself up (well, as much as long-haired rock dudes can spruce themselves up) and he looked cheerful. She felt relieved that she still had a rush of affection for him.

"Jan," he said, in a way which suggested he was after something.

She looked up from her wine glass and saw he had produced something from his pocket.

"We've been together all these years and we've been through so much. I know I'm not always the most romantic type, but I love you," (and he hesitated) "and I thought it was time I asked you to be my wife. Will you marry me?"

He stopped short of getting down on one knee – and it was a low-key proposal – but Janine knew it must have taken some planning and courage. This was someone who would often show his feelings and speak words of love during a night of drunken passion, but never in such a staged setting. Normally he would show his feelings with actions: by fixing and mending stuff around the house. Janine's heart melted at the sight of his expectant face, engagement ring shining in its little box in front of her.

"Of course I will," she whispered.

Chapter Fourteen

Sunday morning, nothing to eat. Need to make sure that tummy was really flat.

What to wear? Black, obviously – but what? Something plain and pretty, that one with the guitar on the front etched in silver and a little bit of lace around the short sleeves. That was a firm favourite. Janine always felt good in that one.

Ruffle up the hair, check eye make-up, looking good.

Engaged to be married.

Janine and Alex had discussed a register office wedding; none of that fluffy, white meringue stuff for her. The ceremony would be followed by a rock party at a local venue. No date had been set, but they were thinking about six months' time. And she was looking forward to it. She had already made several phone calls that morning to let friends and family know. This was the man she really loved – but she was also desperate for 2pm to arrive right now.

She waved the kids off as they got into her ex husband's car. She gave them extra big hugs as they would be away for a week instead of the usual weekend. It was half term so they were going on holiday with their dad and grandparents.

She went back into the flat, missing the boys already. Alex had set off earlier to help his mate fix his car. That was typical of him – ever practical – helping out other people and expecting nothing in return. What a lovely guy. She appreciated him because he was someone who understood her and took care of her every need.

Dion. What a lovely name. He was also someone who understood her and could take care of her every need.

'I'll play it cool', Janine reasoned with herself. 'I can't let him see how I feel. 'Play it cool and just see.'

But as she drove onto the car park at the Arts Centre all sense of 'cool' totally evaporated. She checked herself out in the car mirror. Looking good. Add a touch more lipstick. And a knock on the side window jolted her out of her thoughts.

"Hi," Dion said softly and cheerfully.

Janine fiddled frantically, trying to put the lipstick away, feeling as if she had already been caught out.

"Hi," she answered, trying to sound casual with heart thumping. Oh God. She hoped that somehow he would not look as beautiful today, that the temptation would evaporate. But this time he was wearing tight black jeans tucked into buckled boots and a short black sleeveless T shirt that revealed his muscular upper arms and rode up his back as he leaned forward on the car.

This was not someone who would even consider working out at a boring gym. But he was constantly lugging heavy gear around for the band, rehearsing and performing (and unable to sit down for more than two minutes) so was strong and fit.

"Everyone's looking forward to meeting you. They obviously know all about the Mistress magic," he said directly (without raising his eyes to the heavens like most people did). And the straightforward way he said it made Janine think he really believed in her.

"Come on, I'll introduce you. It's a bit nerve wracking walking in on your own, isn't it?"

Could he really not only be stunning to look at, but nice as well?

Janine attempted to stick to her plan – to feign nonchalance.

"Thanks. I've been really looking forward to it. Should be great," she said as casually and as coolly as she could, but already as they walked through the side door of the rehearsal room his arm was around her protectively and she was aching to put her arm around his slim waist.

"Everybody, this is Janine," he announced.

They were all there, setting up the equipment. And the twin girls she remembered from the Enot's gig were there looking stunning as usual. Everyone made her feel welcome and she revelled in being back in a rehearsal room with all the chaos and light-hearted banter.

"I remember you from the Battle of the Bands at Enot's," Janine said to the twins. "You were awesome. I think my ex band members wanted to poach you."

"Your ex drummer rang me", one the girls said, "but we're happy to stay where we are. And who knows? With you on board, we could go places. We all figured you can't be banned from performing if you are with a completely different set of people, right? Mistress was banned – but you weren't."

Janine liked them all already. The drummer Tommy, a big guy with a mean tattoo and bald head, was actually a softy; the lead/rhythm guitarist Rick, was lean and scrawny, tanned, with straight black hair, so long it stretched right down his back and he was more than a match for Des performance-wise; the bass player, Joey, had a kind of boy next door look with short spiky blond hair and was the obligatory 'quiet one' of the band.

"What say we start with an old standard? See how we gel?" Dion suggested. "How about *Johnny B Goode*?"

The song was wordy, but Janine was more than familiar with the Chuck Berry classic as it was one of her favourites. She nodded, trying to look cool, as if nothing fazed her – but the thought of standing next to him was already driving her crazy. And there appeared to be no girlfriend present. 'Oh God, what if he's gay'? she thought in one horrified moment as the drummer crashed out the intro to the song.

Deep down in Louisiana close to New Orleans ...

And she was beside him, sharing the microphone, breathing his breath, smelling his aftershave, making eye contact, sharing the lyrics, head banging together, laughing together. And their voices in harmony were magic.

The band members romped through another classic, '*Summertime Blues*' with Janine.

Then she sat out for a while to familiarise herself with the music as the band members rehearsed their original Son of Gabriel songs. She was astounded that just three musicians could make such a wall of sound and captivated by the expertise of Rick, whose guitar seemed like an extension of himself.

She watched Dion intently as he performed with natural ease, energy and mock aggression. After hearing the songs a couple of times she joined in where she felt confident, harmonising where possible. And – oh bliss – the drummer was positioned far enough away for her to be able to hear the vocals. Janine felt the rehearsal was going well; she just prayed the others thought so too.

After a couple of hours rehearsing it was taken for granted that she was 'in'. There was no particular discussion between members. Dion simply invited her to the next rehearsal three days later, gave her a tape of the songs to learn and asked her to perform with him at the band's next gig, on home territory at the Arts Centre, in three weeks.

Janine's excitement was mixed with a tinge of fear. Any recurrence of phenomena could mean the end of this wonderful band which was putting its trust in her. Even worse, it could signal the end of performing with Dion. Even worse than that – it would prove that Janine was indeed the source of 'the problem'.

She helped the band pack away the gear; she was used to that and enjoyed the familiar routine. As she waved everyone off in the car park, Dion hesitated before getting into his car, looking troubled, as if he was fighting himself, desperate to say something but trying not to.

"See you Wednesday," he said without looking at her. "You did great, by the way." As he opened his car door he stopped, still, with his back to her and his body language again showed some inner torture going on. It was as if he didn't want to get in the car.

"Dion?" Janine said and walked over to him, but he didn't respond or turn round. "Dion?" She put her hand tenderly, flat against his back, feeling the warmth of his body through his T shirt. "What is it?"

There was no answer in words, but he turned round – and before either of them had even realised it they were together. The kiss was so long and lingering and gentle and soul-reaching that they both knew at that moment, they were meant to be. Even pausing for a second was like tearing two magnets away from each other.

They were both sweaty from the rehearsal session, but the mix of sweat, perfume and aftershave only seemed to heighten the experience.

This was not Janine. She did not do this. She had never in her life thrown herself so readily into the arms of anyone so quickly, least of all have thoughts of taking things further.

"Get in the car," he said with determination and a kind of breathlessness in his voice. He drove without speaking, holding her hand whenever he could by driving one-handed. He pulled the car into the rear car park of the ancient George Hotel just minutes away. Dion gave her a long, direct look that said it all. It said, 'I want you so badly, but if you want to say 'no' say it now'.

There was no need for either of them to say anything. They got out of the car and walked hand in hand into the hotel. Janine watched him as he stood at the reception desk, aching for him, as he booked a room.

They left that room three days later.

Chapter Fifteen

The last time Janine and Dion had rehearsed together they knew virtually nothing about each other. Now, as they walked hand in hand from the hotel to the car, they felt as if they knew everything about each other – everything.

They were tearing at each other's clothes the second they closed the hotel door. They had made love and talked and made love and talked and made love and talked, pausing only to drink and eat a little (courtesy of room service), to sing and use the bathroom.

Any fears that Janine had about ruining the relationship by getting into bed with him were unfounded. They came out of that hotel room with such an intense love that they were prepared to stand defiantly before the world and face the inevitable backlash. In fact, had it not been for the rehearsal being due that day, they probably would have not left the room at all.

Janine marvelled at Dion, stretched out across the duvet. She had caressed every contour of his body and he had done the same to her. She now knew his deepest secrets – even down to his tattoo. She had never been someone who liked tattoos, because of their permanency, but she had laughed out loud as he revealed his secret tattoo which read 'kiss my ass' – on his ass. So she did as the tattoo asked, several times.

He had also traced and re-traced every contour of her, at night and during the day, running his fingers over her until he knew every perfection and imperfection and loved them all the same.

She was stunned to discover that apart from a few dalliances and one night stands, he had only experienced one long-term relationship, which foundered after two years when he discovered she was cheating. Far from living the life of a sex god rock and roll singer, that was not his character. Instead he confessed he was usually last in the queue when it came to girls. The girls saw him as 'too pretty', much preferring the short haired or bald, muscle-bound, manly types. No, it was the Tommy, the drummer, who pulled all the girls.

On the last night at the hotel Dion confessed he had told Tommy at the Enot's gig, when he first set eyes on Janine, 'I'm going to have her'.

Janine wasn't sure whether to feel flattered or offended, because over the last three days he did 'have' her, many times. She feared she had been 'had' – meaning tricked – until he added the words 'for keeps'.

In the hotel room he taught her his band's songs, so she would be word perfect for the Son of Gabriel rehearsal. They sat on the bed singing, harmonising – in tune with each other on the bed and in it. Dion had already taken to calling her 'Jan' and teased her gently by calling her 'my mistress'.

They talked about the Mistress phenomenon into the middle of the night, lying in the darkness. Janine felt a tingle of excitement just hearing his views. He was quite spiritual – the total opposite of Alex who would instantly dismiss any such things as 'a load of crap'.

But Dion was not dismissive of what had happened at the Mistress gigs and he had his own theories. For Janine, it was the first time she felt she had a soul mate to really share her story with.

Dion had been at two of her gigs and he knew something extraordinary HAD happened.

"I think," he said softly in the night. "That sometimes, things align, you know, like stars and planets. Things happen in life that you can't account for in the normal way and they are not always consequences.

"Even in quantum physics extraordinary things happen that very few people ever see. There are new creations, collisions that create amazing new particles. Some things are meant to be. And they are woven in time. Things happen when they are supposed to – like us meeting at the cathedral."

Then he laughed at himself, for sounding so deep.

"Not bad for a guy who just works in a music shop, huh?"

On the first morning they spent together, Dion made an awkward phone call – to his boss. Without giving an explanation he just pleaded for three days unpaid leave, saying he had something urgent he needed to sort out. Janine could tell from his end of the conversation that he must have a good relationship with the boss who agreed to his request without too many questions. She watched Dion run his fingers through his hair – a simple action which he never realised he was doing, but it was one which Janine found so sexy. He ended the conversation with a heartfelt 'Thank you so much. I'll explain everything when I see you'.

Talking into the night, they exchanged stories about strange occurrences which they had both experienced. She told him about the 'velly solly' incident and about the horrible clown picture – excited to even be able to have such conversations.

"And once, I was planning a trip to America," she told him. "I had saved really hard for two years, doing any work I could, often three jobs so I could follow my dream and visit the States."

She told him how she paid for the entire trip, taking her ex husband and two kids, who were very small at the time, with her.

"But the day before I was due to travel," she said, "I was having a coffee with my neighbour – my best friend Helen – when we heard this loud drumming. At the time I lived in a small house on this nondescript, new housing estate nowhere near any main roads. Me and Helen looked at each other as if to say, 'What the—'

"Anyway, we went outside – and there in the road was a small group of what I can only describe as American Indians. They were banging a drum and dancing in the road near my house. We went out and asked them what they were doing and they said they were on some kind of tour. I asked them where they were from and they said Denver in Colorado – exactly where I was travelling to the next day!

"How in God's name is that normal? Why would they be in such an out of the way place? It was like a spiritual, celebratory send-off for me.

"And once, I felt compelled to get a particular book from the library about a psychic medium. I spent all day reading it, immersed in his life – only to hear that night he had died earlier in the day.

"The same happened when I was thinking about a particular song by a rock and roll star. I actually looked up the lyrics – then found out he had died that day.

"And then, a few years ago, when we had a family problem I said a silent prayer as we drove to my sister's house. 'I need some help', I said. 'If there is anyone listening please show me a sign.'

"I remember struggling to suggest something. Looking at the hedgerows as we sped along the road I asked randomly to see two butterflies.

"How stupid. Two butterflies? I was bound to see them anyway. It was summer time, for God's sake. When I got to my sister's, I was sitting in her garden when her little girl came running out to me and dropped something in my lap then ran off laughing. Two wooden butterflies. I asked my sister where they had come from but she swore she had never seen them before.

"Then for about five years afterwards I saw two butterflies every single day: painted on the side of vans, real ones sitting on the wheel of my car in the driveway, two butterflies painted on someone's bag standing in front of me in the queue in the bank, on birthday cards, coffee mugs, shoes, everywhere.

"I remember going to a psychic evening and the medium, who knew me, said: 'Something told me to wear this tonight.'

"It was a T shirt with two kittens on it. But it wasn't the kittens that caught my eye. It was the two butterflies they were chasing.

"On another occasion at work I mentioned the butterfly thing, and even as I spoke, I noticed a picture had been put on my desk – of two butterflies.

"I went to visit an old guy I know who had bought a special tent-like, see-through contraption to put over his vegetable patch in his garden. He told me proudly it kept all insects out. I told him there were two butterflies flying around in it. He wasn't best pleased.

"What are the odds of those things? What is going on?"

Dion then relayed how he remembered a craze sweeping his school. Kids started using a ouija board until it was banned by the staff. But he also remembered a game they used to play: they would lie a pupil on the classroom floor, with six classmates crouched around her: one at the head end, one at the feet and two pupils at either side.

"We used to try and lift a pupil using just two fingers and of course it never worked. But when we tried again, using this particular chant, starting with the person at the head and working our way round three times, we were able to lift the person up easily with just two fingers each. I remember once we lifted Suzanne in the science room high above our head and she was still rising – until she freaked and went crashing to the ground.

"You see, I was levitating people before you!" he said with a laugh.

Janine did not even ask him what the chant was, not wishing to invite anything untoward, and he did not offer to tell her. But she had no doubt that he was telling the truth.

"And I tell you something else," he offered. "You know, when you watch a magic show – particularly with these new

112

magicians who do ridiculously spectacular 'illusions' as they call them. I don't think they are illusions."

"What – you think they're real?" Janine asked staring into his soulful eyes without a hint of mockery.

"I do," he answered seriously. "But, and I've never told anyone this before, I don't think the magician is responsible for the illusion, no more than you were responsible for what happened at your gigs. I just think there are certain people that" – he struggled for the right words) –"things just 'happen around.

"What would an illusionist do? Tell the press? Look ridiculous? No, surely it's far easier to put on a show and trust the illusion will happen," he went on. "Isn't that what happens with psychic mediums? Not the charlatans, but the genuine ones. They can't rehearse their demonstration night can they? They just have to trust it will happen."

"But there's a Magic Circle. They tell their secrets to each other about how the tricks work," Janine said.

"Do they, Jan?" Dion answered. "Or do they just agree to keep the truth amongst themselves?"

Then he went back to his idea of music having some part to play in the Mistress phenomenon.

"I've given a lot of thought about music since your story came out," he said. "Stuff can happen because of huge planets or tiny particles – so why not because of music? Think about it, Jan. There are all these people at a gig, all under one roof, all with one consciousness for that couple of hours, all living in the moment, not just listening to the music, but feeling it. We both know we do what we do because music moves you somehow, it touches your soul.

"Could there be something about that – oneness – that unique moment when everyone, from whatever background, whatever their character, good people or not, share the same experience? Could it be that so many diverse people focussed 'as one' actually makes something happen?"

Janine knew exactly what he meant and felt something stir inside her, the fear she had experienced at the Mistress phenomena.

"What if you're right?" she whispered. "What if we can make things happen?"

"We can," he whispered. "We can make good things happen. Come on, enough of this stuff. It's cold. Come and be my mistress under the duvet."

And they snuggled into the warmth of each other, desire rising with every breath and caress.

On the first night at the hotel, Janine had also made an awkward phone call. She phoned Alex to say she would be away for a while.

"I can't explain right now," she had told a genuinely perplexed Alex. "I'll call you in a couple of days. I think all this talk about getting married has really freaked me. I'm sorry. I'll call you. I need some time to think about things."

And she had put the hotel phone down without giving him the chance to talk any more – feeling like the most ungrateful bitch from hell. She hadn't really lied; just omitted things. She hated herself for being so deceitful and for giving him such a lame story. But she was genuinely freaked by the situation. How could she do this to someone she loved so much that she was about to marry? She could not bear the thought of looking into his hurt eyes. She had taken Alex's engagement ring off her finger and put it safely into her bag, feeling somehow that by taking it off it lessened the crime.

For now, the only course of action was avoidance but she knew the day of reckoning would come.

After three days in the hotel, and still wearing the same clothes they had worn when they walked in there, Janine and Dion walked hand in hand into the Art Centre rehearsal room. In truth it was the first time those clothes had been worn since they were taken off.

Janine allowed herself a small smile, imagining the reaction of Cllr Dorothy Huff if she ever found out about their sex marathon at a Lichfield hotel.

Last time they had walked into the Arts Centre hall, Dion had a protective arm around her, which had looked casual, natural, the thing to do when you introduce someone to a group of people for the first time.

But this time he held her hand tightly and gave it a reassuring squeeze as they walked in. All eyes turned towards them and it was immediately obvious. They may just as well have had a neon sign above their heads, saying, 'We are so much in love'.

"Hi," Dion said as casually as he could. "Everyone OK? Just to let you know – Janine and her kids are moving in with me."

Janine looked as stunned as everyone else.

Chapter Sixteen

"Of course you know he's only with you because you can get publicity for his band?" Alex said angrily as Janine packed her stuff into two giant bags.

She had told him about Dion, but he had already guessed. He'd made some enquiries in the band circles about who was in Son of Gabriel and he knew the type she would go for – a Joey Tempest lookalike from the band Europe. Janine avoided his gaze as much as she could and didn't retaliate when he shouted. He was the victim here after all – and he was too angry to be upset.

He had found out where Dion lived and driven round to his flat, part of a large old house in the nearby town of Burntwood. Janine thanked her lucky stars that Dion had chosen not to take her back home for those first three days, perhaps for that reason.

"I hear he looks like a right girl, a skinny man-child," he sneered. "His hair is longer than yours, for Christ's sake. Well, now you really have had 'em all: the drummer, bass player, rhythm guitarist and now the fucking singer. Hope you're proud of yourself."

This used to be their 'in-joke', only now it didn't seem as funny.

"I'm sorry," was all she could say over and over, dropping things in her hurry to leave and not prolong the agony.

"I'll pick the kids up when they get back. I'll ring their dad and ask him to drop them off at Helen's. I'll need to come back to pick some of their stuff up.

"You need to get back into a band; give yourself some focus," she said lamely but out of genuine concern for him.

As she went out of the door she remembered the ring in her bag.

"I'm sorry, I'm so sorry," she said as she placed it in his hand.

"Fuck you," he said as he threw it on the floor outside. "Oh, no, that's what he's doing," he added sarcastically as he slammed the door behind her.

Janine drove away without looking back. She could only think how that word didn't seem right for the precious nights she had spent with Dion.

Just an hour before going to collect her things, Son of Gabriel had finished the rehearsal. Dion had taught her well so she had managed to get through all of their songs. For two hours they worked hard on the set, putting aside their feelings so as not to feel separate from the rest of the band. Apart from the occasional shared glance, which spoke volumes, they managed to act their way through the songs – pretending to be nothing other than hard-ass rock singers.

Son of Gabriel's music was even heavier and more complex than she was used to in Mistress, but she loved it all the more for that and she was delighted that she was offered the chance of contributing to the song writing. That was, after all, what she did best. She was already brimming with ideas, inspired and feeling really alive for the first time since the collapse of her band.

After the rehearsal, in the car park Dion held onto Janine as if it would be the last time he would see her.

"Be careful," he whispered. "I'm scared you won't come back. Once you see him, you might change your mind."

And he interlinked his fingers with hers as he leant into her car "I'll be at the flat. You've got the address? See you in what – an hour or two?"

But he looked crushed, desolate, convinced she would not be back.

"I'll be there," she said. "Have the wine waiting for me."

And Dion seemed to hold on to her fingers for the longest time possible as she pulled away from him.

"I love you, Jan," he whispered.

It was the first time he had told her, though she already knew it.

"I love you, Dion Rock Star," she said, and missed him already as she drove away.

Chapter Seventeen

Dion led Janine around his rented flat like an excited puppy. It was quite small overall, but had two double bedrooms – and a large lawned area at the rear. 'Perfect for the kids', Janine thought to herself.

He had already started moving stuff out of the second bedroom, his 'junk room' as he called it, to make way for the kids' things and had spent the last hour or so tidying and cleaning ready for her to arrive. But it was obvious the flat was normally immaculate anyway. He would not have had enough time to make it look so pristine. Dion proudly showed her his acoustic and electric guitars, stereo set up, walk-in wardrobe and his shelves full of a range of books from classic to autobiographies and spiritual matters.

Janine just prayed he was ready for his life to be turned upside down by taking on an instant family. But he was ready; in fact he was lonely – at least in his home life. He led a full life and was always surrounded by people, day and night but slept alone. People liked to be around him; he was the stereotypical person who 'lit up the room' when he arrived and made everyone laugh. But he had broken up with his girlfriend and there was no-one special who shared his bed. His parents were living in Spain. Life was work, drinking with mates and making music with the band.

He was a natural with the kids, with the right mix of patience, fun and a firm word for an eleven and fourteen-year-old when necessary. Dion and Janine put their passion aside when the kids were around. Their 'us' time was at night in the bedroom and from Friday night to Sunday night when the boys were with Janine's ex.

Janine had returned to the flat she had shared with Alex on a couple of occasions, but made sure his van was not outside. She had crammed the boot of her MG with as much as she could, then on her last visit, shoved her key through the door with a note, simply saying, 'Sorry'.

Although taking centre stage as singer, Dion was actually an accomplished guitarist. So, weekends were spent song-writing together at the flat, recording the material and rehearsing with the band.

Dion and Janine wrote their first song together one night, with the help of two bottles of wine when the boys were in bed. They wanted a 'power ballad' – an anthem if you like – one that reflected all the stuff they had talked about. Dion came up with a heavy, soul-stirring riff of epic proportions which sliced through the air from the practice amp, while Janine scribbled whatever his music suggested.

Magic of Rock
(to be sung with much theatrics)

For this moment in time your ass is mine
We are gathered here to stand and revere
And wherever you're from and whoever you are

Together we'll feel that rock magic is real.
There's a space in your soul, which can be made whole
There's something deep down inside – if you open your eyes

Chorus
Rock on forever
Wake up, come alive
The magic of rock will
Make you survive

And bad-ass or saint, all can be free
To find more than what we're told to see
We can make it happen, at least we can try
Or we may as well, just lie down and die

When all is done and you're on your own
There is something you take home –
When your lives are ripped apart
There's a magic of rock, lying deep in your heart
Repeat chorus x2

They performed the song to the band at the next rehearsal and it quickly came together with an impromptu jam session, which they recorded. Janine smiled as Dion went into rock star mode for the first line – shaking his fist to the imaginary audience for 'Your ass is mine'.

He also screamed out, 'Rock on' in an ear-shattering pitch, his trademark being able to 'scream in tune'.

It was as if he had two characters: hard-ass rock star and gentle guy. But a part of that gentle being was a quiet determination: Dion was single-minded in the extreme, with an insatiable energy. Dion always got what he wanted.

If people were out of his life it was because he wanted it that way.

With the backing girls on the chorus, the song sounded awesome. And singing the last line, Dion and Janine allowed themselves eye contact which made the song even more powerful.

With Janine's debut appearance with Son of Gabriel due to take place shortly, her anxiety levels grew. There were several things that troubled her: would the press cotton on and do their usual hatchet job, ruining everything before it even started? Would she be rubbish on the night and, worst of all, let Dion down? Would anything untoward happen as she performed with this new line-up or was that all in the past, something that was unique to Mistress? Would she screw up the harmonies on the new epic, *Magic of Rock*?

Dion was adamant that if anything did happen it would be something to celebrate, something good. Ever encouraging, he constantly highlighted the positive aspects of her performance, something Janine wasn't used to.

"I love you, Mistress Jan," he told her several times every day, usually followed by a smile and whisper of, "Kiss my ass."

"I love you, Dion Rock Star," was the usual response and she prayed it would always be like this, that they would never lose this closeness, on or off stage.

Word had got around Lichfield that Son of Gabriel would be performing with new lead vocalist Janine Lee. But the band members had unanimously decided there would be no pre publicity about her debut and that no reference would be made to Mistress before or during the performance. Contrary to what Alex believed, they had wanted Janine for her vocals, not for what had reportedly gone on around her.

The band's posters and advert in the local press rock column simply read:

ROCK OUT WITH
SON OF GABRIEL
LIVE AT LICHFIELD ARTS CENTRE
AUGUST 31st 9pm

Janine also made a conscious decision to change her image. Out went the black leather mini skirt, waistcoat and thigh-length boots. She decided to complement her Adonis front man, who wore black with flashes of red on stage, by wearing the same colours – only her outfit was more rock feminine. She needed to wear something that allowed freedom of movement, so she chose a simple black mini dress, low cut, showing an ample cleavage. She teamed this up with a wide red, studded belt, short black fringed boots, red leather wrist bands and black tights. She washed her hair and deliberately made it look dishevelled. Impressive though her long locks were, they were outdone by Dion's which tumbled down his back naturally, without him having to do anything other than get in and out of the shower.

The night arrived and Janine was relieved there had been nothing about her in the press prior to the performance. The band members all sat in a quiet area which had been set aside for them in the bar an hour before the performance. There was a rock disco blaring, the place was packed and the punters were already in high spirits. Dion interlinked his fingers with hers, his usual way of showing support, something he often did now if he sensed she needed any comfort. There was no need for words. Just feeling his hand squeeze hers was enough.

Then she spotted him: Greyman had walked into the bar.

She turned away quickly, hoping he hadn't seen her – a futile action anyway since he had obviously turned up for the performance. But she did not want to speak to him beforehand. The rest of the band members saw him too, but only the drummer reacted - with one word. "Wanker."

The band had come up with their own intro tape: very drum-driven, like a thumping heartbeat that sped up as they were about to take to the stage. In the back ground was a simple but dramatic keyboard sound, just three notes but effective all the same.

That night as the drumming quickened in the intro tape, so did Janine's heart. This was it; taking care of business; back where she belonged. They made their way to the stage among a catcall of whistles and beer-y cheers. Dion and Janine were no longer a couple; they were performers, part of a band – for the next hour or so at least.

Greyman was at the back of the hall. Janine wondered why he came at all since he hated heavy music so much.

On cue the band launched into its first song, and with four vocalists, the audience was hit by a wall of sound.

Dion, rock star, as opposed to Dion, lover, was in the moment. He was in command, fearless, confident, well-rehearsed and a natural. He was aggressive, inciting the first few rows into a frenzy. And all this made it easy for Janine to act the part too. There were no smiles allowed, no niceties, just an edgy performance, giving the punters what they had come to hear.

No reference was made to Janine as a new band member until half way through the set when the new song made its debut. The lights were dimmed and Dion, rock star commanded his audience to be quiet - and they obeyed, however tough they thought they were.

"This is a new song, written by our new vocalist Jan." Cheers and wolf whistles from the crowd. And then, and only then, did he allow himself to glance at her – and there was a hint of pride in his eyes, which only she saw, as he kept up his badass persona for the audience.

"Join in on the chorus."

And he spoke the words for them before the song started, delivering them in actor-like voice with attitude:

Rock on forever
Wake up, come alive
The magic of rock will
Make you survive

The band launched into the opening bars of the song with the lights dimmed low and Dion enjoyed his 'your ass is mine' moment – shaking clenched fist at the audience with his right hand while grabbing Janine's ass with his other.

Greyman winced.

But as far as everyone else was concerned it was going great.

The audience did as they were told. A little hesitant over the words at first, they joined in on the chorus and by the time it was repeated twice at the end they were word perfect.

Rock on forever

Wake up, come alive
The magic of rock will
Make you survive

But what Dion and the band did not realise was the words were projected onto the blank wall behind them. The audience reaction was so amazing that Dion indicated for the rest of the band to stop playing while he let the audience take over. They sang it, arms aloft for a third time, a fourth time, a fifth time   each time getting louder and singing with more meaning. It was an anthem.

Then some of them got the timing a little out of synch, but the results were soul stirring. It reminded Dion of songs he used to sing at school: *Frere Jacques* or *London's Burning* with the class singing it in a round; as one section of the audience started the chorus, another part of the crowd came in later. And they kept it going on and on and on.

A searchlight swept over the audience, every now and then fixing on individuals bawling out the chorus, whether they could sing or not.

He stood at the front of the stage with microphone outstretched and listened in genuine amazement. It was one of those moments to savour and he dropped the hard rock persona to laugh and enjoy the moment.

But after about eight choruses he turned and signalled to the band to come back in. It was only when he turned round that he noticed the chorus projected onto the wall.

He nodded to Janine indicating that she should look behind her and he mouthed, "What the f—?"

But Janine had to concentrate on the job at hand: she joined in the anthem with the twins until Dion gave his sign for the band to wind up and the drummer crashed in for a sudden end. The applause was rapturous.

Only Greyman stood with his arms down, grim faced, feeling nothing.

"OK. Shut the fuck up now and get ready to rock!" he commanded and signalled to the band to launch into the next song – an up tempo, heavy song with no nonsense lyrics which did the trick.

The audience moshed together, crowd surfed and pogod up and down as if their lives depended on it. The band put everything into making the rest of the set as edgy as possible, earning a resounding two encores at the end.

"What fucking searchlight?" Dion said to Janine as they ran off the stage after the last encore, covered in sweat. "No one here has a searchlight."

Back in the quiet area of the bar some of the punters were making their way to the band. Janine watched as Dion embraced them, whether they were guys or girls. He was a very tactile person, with natural exuberance, which she found fascinating; always there with a hug for everyone, arms around their shoulders, a 'high five' or a man love fist bump.

"Great gig," one leather-clad biker yelled at them. "Dunno what you did there but I'm feelin' it, man," he said as he punched at the area where he supposed his heart would be – but way off target.

The band members were all on a high (on a high on music that is, as opposed to drugs). As far as Janine knew none of the band was into the drug scene; they drank until they were silly and funny and all the guys except for Dion smoked, but that was it. The band were congratulating Janine on getting through the first gig when she turned to

Dion and whispered, "Think it's best I don't write any more songs for the band."

"No, it was great," he said. "I dunno what it was about that chorus, but it felt really powerful. We should write some more." And he groaned as he saw Greyman approach him.

"That promoter Miles rang me today," Greyman announced self-importantly to the band. "He's heard your stuff. Someone sent him one of your CDs and he wants to manage the band – especially now he's heard you've got Janine. Seems he's already arranged a record contract." (He said this with a 'God knows why' expression). "He asked me to give you his new number."

Greyman handed a piece of paper to Dion and left without saying anything about the gig – he saved that for newsprint. But little did Greyman realise he would have more to write about in next week's paper than he bargained for.

"What about what happened in there tonight?" the drummer said. "Freakin' weird if you ask me. This is Mistress again all over. An invisible searchlight? Words on a wall? And that reaction to the new song? What the hell was that all about?"

The other band members looked uncomfortable that he had brought it up but after some discussion, they decided they had half expected it with Janine on board.

"Nothing bad happened tonight, right?" Dion said to the band, stuffing the phone number into his jeans pocket. "Let's go for it." And they all drank to that.

Chapter Eighteen

Weary, but happy, the band members hauled their gear out through the side doors of the Arts Centre. There were only a few stragglers left, and a couple of them volunteered to help. The band members all had one thing in mind: that their time had come, they had paid their dues performing on the local circuit for two years and now someone had taken notice, for whatever reason. They all wanted to go places – and they were ready.

Dion was in high spirits fuelled by alcohol, news of a record contract and at the amazing way the gig had gone. He was also looking forward to getting between the sheets with his 'mistress'. Janine laughed at him as he dropped his jeans in the car park for her, mooning in the moonlight, just enough to reveal his 'kiss my ass' – an invitation for later – then with a meaningful grin pulled them up quickly again.

Then someone called his name, a familiar voice. Dion turned round and Janine watched as two men came out from the shadows like silhouettes. And it all seemed to happen so quickly. One raised his arm and she heard a sickening crunch as a metal bar came crashing down onto Dion's head.

Then they were out of shadows, Alex and his mate Nick, clearly drunk and very angry.

Dion was already on the floor and even in the darkness Janine could see a pool of dark fluid seeping from his head across the car park.

"That's for Alex," Nick yelled. "And this is from me, you bastard," he said as he continued hitting him with the bar as he lay on the ground. Alex waded in, kicking him repeatedly. Janine could not believe her eyes as this was someone she had never even heard raise his voice.

She heard a voice screaming Dion's name in the distance, a voice she didn't recognise at first, but as reality clawed its way through her shocked brain she realised it was her own. Alex and Nick had fled, perhaps because of Janine's screams bringing it home to them what they had done. She was on her knees, screaming for someone to get an ambulance, shaking and desperately trying to stop the flow of blood which had turned Dion's blond hair red.

She knelt on the cold concrete, gently lifting Dion's head onto a rolled up coat which someone brought over to her. One of the twins gave her a towel which Janine pressed as hard as she could against his head.

Tommy the drummer, who had given chase to Alex and Nick, came back breathless; they were nowhere to be seen. They had fled in the direction of Beacon Park, a vast area with so many places to hide in the darkness. Tommy was ranting, furious, breathing hard and at one point actually screamed out to the night sky in his anger.

Now talking softly, Janine cradled Dion's head in her hands, pleading with him to be OK. She knew he had had no time to defend himself. She tried to keep the blood away from his eyes and could just about make out in the half light that his eyes were open. She put one hand up the front of his T shirt and rested it on his chest. She could feel he was breathing, but he was quiet, so quiet, so unlike Dion.

"The ambulance is coming," she told him quietly. "Just lie still, I'm here. You're going to be OK. You're going to be OK. You're going to be OK," then screamed tearfully to the others, "Bring me something to keep him warm. Where's the ambulance?"

She touched his face and the blood on her hands left smears on his cheeks. She looked into his eyes, still open, but somehow not right.

"Stay with me, stay with me. Talk to me, talk to me."

"I'll be OK," he said quietly without moving or blinking. She took his hand and he interlinked his fingers into hers, squeezing them tightly to reassure her, then closed his eyes.

She could hear a siren in the distance. The grip which Dion had on her hand had already fallen away.

Chapter Nineteen

It reminded Janine of a cheap movie: the ambulance, the corridors, the shouting voices in Accident and Emergency, the weeping relatives and the disembodied feeling that this was not really happening.

Dion was taken from her and she was left desolate in a waiting room in the early hours of Sunday morning.

The staff had crowded round him, using medical terms she did not understand. The ambulance men had performed a handover, informing the A & E staff of what had happened. All she could do was wait. The rest of the band arrived. No-one spoke, but everyone's eyes betrayed their worst fears and the twins were openly crying. Janine felt too numb to cry.

"Nothing bad has happened tonight," he'd said. He was happy, clowning around, being himself. And she could not believe that Alex was capable of such a thing, least of all that he could be facing a charge of manslaughter, at least.

The police arrived and the hours passed as she gave a statement, staring ahead, with no emotion, just saying the words, telling them how it happened. This was the last thing she wanted to do, fearful that Alex (who she still perceived as the other victim in all this) would be sent to prison. But lying to the police did not seem an option. She remembered he had an iron bar like the one she saw in the moonlight, which he would often use to jack up his car.

The other band members gave their account, but it was only Janine who had witnessed the attack from the start. After all, she was the one watching him at the time, captivated by his sense of fun, even when he was tired.

Slowly the band members went home, promising to call the following day, until only Tommy was left to stay with her. He may have been the meanest looking member of the band, but he too dissolved into tears when they were on their own.

"I don't know what I'll do if I lose him," she whispered to him. "Did you hear him whisper, he will be OK? Even then he was trying to comfort me."

And she wailed uncontrollably for the next half hour with the drummer awkwardly wrapping his bulky arms around her.

"You go home," she told him at about four a.m. I'll sleep here. I'm not going anywhere."

"You sure you'll be OK? I'm bushed."

And she nodded unconvincingly.

"I'll come back tomorrow," he said. "Ring me if there's any news."

And she fell asleep fitfully, stretched across three hard chairs. Sometime in the night a nurse must have come in because when she woke up she was covered with a blanket and there was a pillow beneath her head.

The horror of the night before immediately engulfed her. She threw off the blanket and left the room, feeling slightly wobbly, desperate to find someone who could give her any news.

A staff member was walking towards her, grim faced, and her heart fell like a stone.

"Are you the girlfriend of Mr Freeman?"

'Mr Freeman', she thought. She could not think of him as anything but Dion.

"Yes. How is he?" she implored, her eyes fixed on the nurse's mouth, wandering whether her life was to be saved or ruined by her next sentence.

"The doctor would like to see you," she said simply and with a hint of pity, Janine thought.

She was led to a small room off the corridor where a doctor invited her in.

"You're Mr Freeman's girlfriend, I believe?" he asked

'Just tell me, just tell me', her head was screaming.

"Please sit down. You are Miss—?"

"Lee. Is he going to be OK?"

'Just tell me, just tell me', her head was screaming.

"I understand his parents are living in Spain," he said, prolonging the agony and making her feel this must be serious.

"Yes. Please tell me if he's OK," she asked, trying not to sound as exasperated as she felt.

"It's difficult to say, I'm afraid, Miss Lee. Your boyfriend is in a coma. He may have suffered permanent brain damage and also has two broken ribs. We have carried out scans but it is impossible to say at this stage what the outcome will be, whether he will survive at all – and if he does, what effect the blows to the head will have had."

'But he's alive', was all Janine could think as the rest of the doctor's words went over her head.

"Miss Lee. Do you understand what I've said? I think we should alert his parents that their son has a life-threatening injury."

'But he's alive now', was all that Janine could think, over and over.

"Yes. Their number will be in his notebook. It's usually in his jacket. I'll ask the band to find it. Can I see him?"

The doctor looked at her matter of factly and without compassion. He had seen it all before.

"We will allow just one visitor today. He is in intensive care, but if you follow me—"

And she was walking into the intensive care room where he lay on life support, surrounded in tubes and wires and beeping machines and drips, with a specialist nurse hovering around him.

Janine sat next to the bed and gently stroked the back of his hand; simply being able to touch him gave her some sense of connection. They had shaved part of his head. His hair, his pride and joy which was always immaculately clean, was a tangled mess with stains of red fading to dark pink. The hospital lights made him look pale. He looked peaceful, but that alarmed Janine rather than comforted her because quiet and peaceful was the opposite of his character. Where was Dion, the one who was always laughing, chatting, singing, swearing and teasing?

Having never met them, Janine felt unable to break the news to his parents so when she tracked down their number she asked if the staff would call them. Their reaction was to book a flight immediately and they were due to arrive the following day.

Janine made a tearful phone call to her ex husband and asked him to keep the boys for a while longer. He was surprisingly nice, actually sounded concerned and told her to 'take care'. She had already decided her place was here, however long that took. In any case she would be too terrified to leave the room for any length of time for fear she would not be there when he woke up or—

The nurse asked if she would like a cup of tea and Janine nodded, aware she must have looked a sight.

"You can talk to him," the nurse said kindly. "That may help both of you."

But each time she tried to speak, a lump rose into her throat, making it impossible to get the words out so she resigned herself to hours of sitting, waiting in a state of anxiety for the slightest flicker of movement.

And as the days went by her anxiety levels heightened.

Dion's parents had arrived quietly into the room. Janine was immediately struck by the likeness he had to his mum. Slim and naturally blond, still beautiful for her age, she was tanned from the Spanish sun.

And his dad, well built with a healthy brown complexion, reminded her of a middle aged former rock dude. His brown hair was worn defiantly with a small pony tail. She could see straight away: here was Dion's appearance and his fun but determined character, wrapped up in both of them.

Janine did not know whether to smile or not as they entered the room; there seemed nothing to smile about, but equally she was meeting his parents for the first time so did not want to appear unfriendly. She attempted a half smile, but it was Dion's dad who broke the ice and wrapped his arms round her as he looked at his son. By doing so, he ensured she could not see the tears which brimmed in his eyes.

His wife, wearing a pretty blouse with two butterflies on it, began to cry quietly and she took her son's hand.

"Hello, love," she said. And at first Janine thought she was speaking to Dion, but she was looking at her.

"I'm so sorry," Janine whispered. "This is my fault. If he hadn't met me—"

"You didn't do this to him," she replied. "He's spoken about you on the phone and I know he loves you very much. I want to thank you for making my boy happy."

"I love your beautiful son," Janine managed to say.

There was nothing more to be said, just silent tears and quiet private thoughts for the next couple of hours as they watched the nursing staff come and go.

It was decided that his parents would move into Dion's flat and visit the hospital every day. Janine was relieved as they told her they would cover all the bills for his home. On top of everything, she did not want him to lose his precious flat.

As days went into weeks a pattern emerged. People would come and go, including the band members and Dion's boss. Janine had called into the music shop a few days before 'the incident' and met him. He was a former musician, middle aged, still with a penchant for dressing in denim and 'cool', she thought, in a good way.

She was keen to see where Dion worked so that when she was at college in the day she could imagine him in his work situation. But work for Dion wasn't so far removed from his life in the band. No wonder he loved his job; he was in his element: demonstrating guitars for customers, giving them advice, jamming with them; drinking copious amounts of coffee; and laughing and chatting with those who just called in because they liked being around other musicians.

Also visiting the hospital as well as his parents were many of his mates, fans of the band – and her boys. For Janine, not seeing her boys was like a triple heartache as she missed them as much as Dion.

Her boys talked nonsense during their visits, but nobody minded. They talked about their friends, their day at school, their bikes and petty scraps to Dion – or 'Dio', as they called him.

When they first met him they decided Dion was 'a girl's name' and despite Janine assuring them the female version was spelt differently, it simply wasn't manly enough, especially for a young teenager to use.

So Janine told them about a rock singer called Ronnie James Dio. Was that bloke-y enough for them? So Dio it was from then on – and he seemed to take it as a compliment, not an insult.

"So Dio, when you come home there's loads of stuff needs fixing. Paul broke my bike—"

"No, I didn't."

"Yes, you did. I told you not to do wheelies on it. Use your own bike—"

"Well you burst my football."

"And you broke the window."

"Anyway, Dio, when you wake up you can see my trophy. Dad took us to a BMX race and I got a first place on the podium—"

And on and on it went; funny and sad at the same time.

If willing something to happen could achieve the impossible, then Dion would have woken up. Janine prayed and cried and cursed and willed it to happen, but two months on there was no response.

All band members were unanimous: there would be no Son of Gabriel without Dion and remarkably, they thought, Miles said he would wait. Miles had travelled all the way from his home in London to visit the hospital, a gesture which Janine appreciated. They sat and talked quietly through various options for the band. No plans could be made yet for performances but Miles was savvy enough to know Dion's situation was a golden opportunity for publicity/money making, even now. He asked Janine about her one and only performance with Son of Gabriel, keen to know if there had been any repetition of 'happenings'. Janine told him about the new song: about the powerful effect the chorus seemed to have on the audience; about the lyrics projected onto the wall; and the searchlights. Mindful that Mistress was banned from venues across the country, she offered to leave the band if he thought she was a problem. Sure, this was her dream, but it was Dion's band and she would never stand in the way of his dream, even if that meant dashing her own ambitions and watching him on stage without her.

Miles told her as long as nothing extreme or dangerous happened he felt they could explain things away as 'illusions' or 'effects', but she thought it odd that he did not try to rationalise what had happened like most people did.

"Dion said only good things will happen when we go on stage," she told him, and had to look away so he would not see her trying to hold back the tears. It was a stark reminder that they may never even get to find out what the future held.

News of Dion's attack had made the local press. Greyman had shelved the spiteful review of the gig which he intended to print and was actually excited to have what he considered a 'real' front page news story to write. And for once he dealt with the band respectfully.

Shock Attack - Singer Left in a Coma

by Alan Greyman

Lead singer of Lichfield rock band Son of Gabriel is in a serious condition after an unprovoked attack on Saturday night.

Dion Freeman, aged thirty-two, from Burntwood, was struck several times with a metal bar and kicked by two men after a performance at Lichfield Arts Centre.

He suffered severe head injuries, broken ribs and remains in a coma.

The popular singer, who was on the brink of securing a recording contract with his band, had performed to a packed house that night.

The attack occurred in the car park as the band, including new member Janine Lee on joint lead vocals, packed away their gear around midnight.

Police say two local men have been arrested and bailed. The police are liaising with the hospital and hope to interview Mr Freeman if and when he recovers.

Lichfield District Council chairman Councillor Dorothy Huff called for the Arts Centre to be closed because of the attack.

'I'm appalled by the violence which took place in our fine city', Cllr Huff said. 'If this is the sort of thing that goes on after these type of events then we should close the venue down.

'My condolences go to this young man and his family'.

At the time of going to press a hospital spokesperson said Mr Freeman's condition remained 'serious'.

The article carried a front page photo, one of the band's publicity shots, of Dion in rock star pose holding the microphone.

The story and photo seemed to have struck a chord with people who were enraged that such a popular local guy could be in this position. The band members brought the papers to Janine each week and she was astounded to see how many publications had picked up on it.

It seemed that pictures of Dion were everywhere – and there were heart-rending letters of support which poured into the press and the hospital. It seemed there were updates every week and even the nationals were picking up the story.

One of the papers had come up with the idea of raising money to pay for Dion's rehabilitation and appealed for ideas. The paper kick started the fund with a thousand pound donation.

One of the fundraising ideas from the band was 'Rock For Dion' – a series of gigs at which local rock bands would be invited to perform. And there followed a series of concerts with bands performing free of charge. All proceeds from the ticket price and bucket collection at the gig were for the cause.

A local shop started producing Rock For Dion T shirts to raise money – black and red, of course. It seemed everywhere you went there were people wearing them with special fundraising wrist bands provided by a Lichfield shop. The wrist bands were black with a flash of red – with the words 'Rock For Dion' printed on them.

People started asking for Son of Gabriel music so the band provided a CD for sale which featured Dion's latest work, the hastily recorded *Magic of Rock*. With a bit of extra work in the studio the anthem sounded awesome.

It could be heard playing at local shops, clubs, bars, at people's homes, on local radio, then national radio, then local TV, then national TV, then international music channels, accompanied by video footage of him.

Dion was a star.

Thousands of pounds were waiting for him in an account hastily set up for the charity and the money was growing day by day.

The demand for the band's music was insatiable and Janine had to constantly turn down interviews, preferring to wait for the day when and if he could join her.

The lump in her throat was gone and she was able to talk freely to Dion now. It gave her a tiny shred of comfort to be able to speak to him, even if there was nothing in return. She read all the newspaper reports out loud to him, played their music and his favourite bands quietly and sat writing new songs, one of them dedicated to Dion called *When you Wake*, but never knowing if they would ever see the light of day. She had written it in such a way that it would be appropriate for male or female vocals – simply about loving someone and watching them while they slept.

When you Wake

As I lie here while you're sleeping,
Picturing your ice blue eyes,
I pray you're in a land of sweet dreams

In a world of sunny skies

When you wake I'll be beside you
As I'm always meant to be
The love I feel for you is so true
Feeling whole means you and me

Chorus (in four part harmony)

I can't sleep at night for lovin' you
I can't sleep at night for lovin' you
Oooooooo, for lovin' you
I can't sleep at night for lovin' you

I can't sleep for lovin' you so
My heart hurts so much it aches
Time is ticking by just too slow
Waiting for you to awake
Chorus

Janine slept in a makeshift bed in Dion's room. He had been moved from intensive care into a specialist unit, but was still in need of constant attention. She kept him clean and smelling sweet, just as he would have wanted. His hair had grown back over the shaved patches and she made sure it was an 'organised mess' each day, his usual image.

"You are a star," she would whisper to him frequently. "You really are Dion Rock Star."

And she would sing their epic *Magic of Rock* chorus to him over and over – stung by the reality of the words.

Rock on forever

Wake up, come alive
The magic of rock will
Make you survive

She could not possibly have known when she wrote those words just how poignant they would become.

As the weeks went by and the band became more and more frustrated by being out of action, it was decided they would hold a 'pretend rehearsal' in Dion's room every Sunday afternoon. That was their normal rehearsal time anyway.

They did not even feel ridiculous playing pretend instruments, air guitaring, drumming on the cupboard, singing all the guitar riffs. It had become the norm. And they even managed to enjoy their 'performances', laughing at their stupid sounds, desperate for Dion to join in.

The staff allowed the fiasco, prepared to try anything which may help get a response.

"Just listen to yourselves," one lovely Irish nurse said at one of their 'rehearsals'. "Six of you, six grown adults, all completely bonkers," and she was laughing as she left the room.

Janine went quiet, then, as if a light bulb had switched on in her head, she leapt to her feet.

"Six of us. Six of us," she said urgently.

The band members looked at her as if the Irish nurse was right. She had gone bonkers.

"Get up. Get up. Tommy, you stand there; Rick, go to the bottom of the bed; Eva and Lou – stand at his side; Joey, stand here with me, this side."

They were all so surprised by her sudden outburst that they did as they were told: one at his head, one at his feet, two either side.

"It's not a coincidence I came up with those words to the chorus," she said convincingly.

"Place two fingers of each hand underneath him." And she said it with such determination that they obeyed. They couldn't see what harm it would do.

And nodding to Tommy at the head of the bed she ordered him, "Repeat after me.

"Rock on forever."

And she nodded to each of the band members in turn so they would repeat the words one after the other like a chant.

Then she said, *"Wake up, come alive."*

No-one spoke, except to repeat what Janine instructed.

"The magic of rock will—"

The words went round a little hesitantly, one by one.

"Make you survive."

"Again," Janine ordered. And they spoke the words around him, one line at a time.

> *"Rock on forever*
> *Wake up, come alive*
> *The magic of rock will*
> *Make you survive"*

They understood where she was coming from now and they spoke with more conviction.

"Again," Janine ordered and her eyes bored into Dion's soul, willing him to wake up.

*"Rock on forever
Wake up, come alive
The magic of rock will
Make you survive"*

And she thought she detected a flicker of the eyelids, but she wanted it so badly she could have imagined it.

"One more time, please," she added, prepared to admit failure and feel a fool.

*"Rock on forever
Wake up, come alive
The magic of rock will
Make you survive"*

And his eyelids did flicker.

"Keep your hands where they are," she said and they all hardly dared to breathe.

Those beautiful blue eyes blinked open slowly. There was no sound from him, no movement of his body, just a gentle reawakening and look of confusion.

Janine moved her fingers from beneath him and the others followed.

"Go and get the nurse," she told one of the twins.

"Dion? Dion?"

There was no response, just a look of bewilderment in his eyes.

"You're in hospital. Do you understand where you are?" Janine asked, concerned that he would be afraid.

And he blinked slowly.

But was Dion really in there? Was the character she loved and longed for so much still able to get through somehow?

"Dion? Say something if you can to let me know you are really here."

And he tried to whisper, but it was weak and quiet.

Janine leant down and put her face next to his. "Say it again," she said gently. And he looked directly into her eyes and whispered to her.

The band members looked alarmed as she burst into tears then realised she was laughing at the same time.

"What did he say?" Tommy asked, his face looking fit to crumble at any minute.

"Kiss my ass," she said stroking Dion's face.

Chapter Twenty

Over the next few days Dion slept, woke for short periods, slept again, woke again. Janine had developed a sixth sense that told her instinctively when he was just sleeping as opposed to falling into a coma, so she no longer worried when he slept.

And during the short periods when he was awake he spoke a little more each time.

Janine felt protective and did not want to stress him by talking about the attack or how he had woken up, but the police had been informed by the staff that Dion was conscious.

"How long have I been out of it?" was how he put it when he managed to stay awake for more than a few minutes.

"Three and a half months," she told him, bracing herself for an expression of hurt and disbelief. "I'm sorry, I know how you usually can't keep still for a minute. That must be hard to find out."

"But I haven't wasted my time," he told her slowly, in the direct manner she still found hard to get used to. "I've been working; I've come up with some amazing riffs and lyrics; you need to get my guitar while they're still in my head."

She sat open-mouthed at his drive even as he lay in bed. Her expression was one which Dion always found amusing – one he saw often in her, as she shook her head and looked incredulous at most things he said or did.

'You need to get my guitar', was a command actually, she realised. He never raised his voice, ever. He never ordered anyone to do anything in an offensive way; he simply made clear what he wanted – and got his way.

The only time he looked tearful was at finding out that she had kept a vigil at the hospital all that time.

"Dion, what's the last thing you remember?" she asked him.

His voice was still quiet and tired, but he managed to say: "I remember everything. And I told you I would be OK, didn't I?"

"The police want to talk to you when you are well enough," she said hesitantly.

"No problem," was the response, without any hint of anxiety.

Over the next few days, Dion's progress was so rapid that it was now the doctors who were shaking their heads in disbelief. 'Miracle' was a word they did not use lightly, but it was one which they applied to Dion's recovery.

Janine asked his parents to bring his acoustic guitar to the hospital, and he was working on riffs before he could even sit up properly, as if it was the perfectly normal thing to do.

His parents, who knew their son, an only child, even better than Janine did, never once suggested to him that he should rest. They were simply ecstatic that their precious son was 'back' doing what he had always done – playing guitar and scribbling down the chords.

When his parents left the room to make their way back to the flat Janine asked him something she was desperate for him to explain. "What did you mean when you said you didn't waste your time?" she asked. "What time? You were completely out of it. How could you be writing songs?"

"I was somewhere else," was all he would say. "I'll talk about it with you when the time is right and we are back in our own bed."

"But how— What else—"

"You reached out to me and I heard, but I couldn't find the way back – so I put the idea of six people and that experience I had at school into your head. I felt your six energies dragging me out. I could have stayed, I was happy there, but I wanted to be back because I have stuff to do with you, so I allowed myself to be pulled free."

"You felt us all 'pulling you back'?"

"Like I said, I'll explain more when I'm ready; when you're on a pillow next to me."

And she knew better than to ask any more questions.

Janine was exchanging information with him little by little, afraid to overload him and he was doing the same with her.

She started to gently mention his fame and the fortune which was growing by the day – and braced herself for a shocked response.

But he simply said, "I know. You read the papers to me every day – and I always knew I would be famous anyway. I'm Dion Rock Star." (Cue open-mouthed reaction and shake of head from Janine again).

His words were not said with conceit, more as a fact.

There was no hint from him that he needed her to explain any further and he never asked any more questions about being famous.

"I need to be in a studio in a couple of months," he announced. "And you will be with me too. I've got new songs to record and we need to work on them together. Tell Miles to book it."

And there was that gentle command again. She had no doubt that he would achieve his goal. He always did. Whatever Dion wanted, Dion got.

Instead of resting he worked on putting music to the words she had written for *When You Wake*, that was his therapy. And he crafted more songs written in his 'other place'.

When he wasn't working on music he told Janine all the things he intended to do to her in no uncertain terms, just as soon as his body caught up with his brain. Yes, he was back.

But his erotic words were said in such a way that they were not offensive to her; more a promise of catching up on the loving nights they had missed out on these past months, and those words travelled straight to parts of her which ached for him to be back in their bed at home.

For now they had to be content on interlinking fingers and lingering kisses when the staff left the room. All Janine could do at night was lie in her bed in the half light, watching him just feet away from her.

When the staff felt he was ready to be interviewed, the police were eventually allowed in. Dion asked Janine to leave him with the two policemen who were to carry out the interview. She sat outside with a coffee and a magazine intending to sit there for at least an hour; she had after all got used to waiting around.

But when the door opened after just ten minutes and the police left looking less than pleased she was puzzled.

"What's going on?" she asked him as he sat propped up with pillows.

"I told them I'm not pressing charges against either of them," he said simply.

"But—"

"I'm not pressing charges. I had it coming; it served me right. I took you from him and I got what I deserved," he said with a shrug.

And she knew better than to even try and persuade him to change his mind. Dion never changed his mind once it was made up.

She could not pretend she did not feel relief, for Alex's sake, but she still found his decision extraordinary.

Weeks of intense private physio, courtesy of the Rock For Dion fund, followed.

As Dion improved, his parents flew back to Spain to free up the flat ready for his return home with Janine and the kids.

Janine had got quite close to his mum and dad, spending so much time at the hospital with them. She found out that the silver bracelet he wore and treasured was a special gift from his mum on his 30th birthday. There were hugs all round as his parents left the hospital for the last time and his mum held Janine close.

"Thank you for giving your wonderful son to the world," Janine said, trying to take the sadness out of his mum's eyes. "It must be really hard for you leaving him behind."

"I'm handing him to you now," she said, "gift wrapped."

'Gift wrapped. What a wonderful expression', Janine thought.

Dion returned home five and a half months after the attack –and the first thing he did was to make good on all the promises he made to her about what he would do to her when they returned home – and more. The pillow talk would come later; for now there was a lot of action to catch up on.

Chapter Twenty-One

Well within Dion's self imposed deadline, the band had recorded the new music and lyrics in the studio and was back on stage.

It was meant to be a try out, low key gig to get him back into performing, but the demand for tickets was so great that instead of being back at the Arts Centre the event was moved to the city's Garrick Theatre.

When it was announced that the gig was also to be recorded live for the first album hundreds of fans queued for tickets around the building as soon as they were released. The performance would be in front of a capacity crowd of six hundred.

Dion had handed in his notice at work as Miles had paid an advance to the band and booked them on a UK tour, with a major European tour to follow – and the stadiums were already selling out, such was the band's reputation which had gone before them.

Janine had given a lot of thought about how to set off on a European tour with two kids and concluded it would not be possible. She would have to quit and join Dion whenever she could, perhaps perform a 'guest appearance' she reasoned. He was the star; it was his picture splashed across every newspaper and magazine because of his story; it was Dion everyone wanted to see. The thought made her uneasy. Dion may not have been promiscuous on home ground – but on tour performing in front of hordes of young rock chicks? She felt as if she had lost him already. But, if it was a choice between Dion and her boys—

So she broached the subject with him before the Garrick Theatre performance. She should have known him better by now. Leaving the band was not even a consideration, he told her: the kids were coming with them; they would hire a tutor; what was the problem?; if you quit I'm not going – and that was that – all delivered in his trademark matter of fact, I am in charge, softly spoken, polite tone with no negotiating and no compromise. End of discussion.

Before the Garrick theatre performance Dion and Janine visited the venue together to check out some queries with the technician. She hadn't noticed it before, but she realised as they walked through the city streets that Dion looked so out of place. Even if he tried to 'dress down' and mingle in, he still stood out from the crowd. People of all ages did a double take as he passed by; he looked like a celebrity without trying. It was as if he had already left this life behind and simply did not belong here. It took an age to reach the theatre because of all the, 'Hi, Dions', 'Glad to have you back', 'How are you'?, 'You look great', etc etc as people stopped to talk. He handled it all with grace and humour, though Janine could tell he just wanted to press on.

Dion got into talking technicalities with the theatre staff so she decided to head to the city to buy some essentials and arranged to meet him at the music shop in half an hour.

She made her way through Tudor Row, a quaint passageway which led to the main shopping area and her heart leapt and sank at the same time. Alex was just coming out of the bank – and he had seen her so there was no avoiding him. After what they had shared she did not want to do that. There was an awkward, 'Hi', and he was decidedly cool.

"How are you?" she asked, genuinely concerned.

"Good. I'm back in a band – a Status Quo tribute – and there's none of that crap happening when we perform. Actually I'm glad I bumped into you; there's a few things I'd like you to hear."

And he looked around as if to say 'not here'.

"You in a hurry? We could stop for a coffee," he suggested.

"OK, yes, it would be good to have a catch up, but I've only got about half an hour."

They made their way to what used to be one of their favourite cafes near to the cathedral, an ancient building with a dining area on two floors. If felt strange walking alongside him and not linking an arm into his.

They made small talk until they reached the cafe then climbed the rickety stairs to the slanted, beamed, tiny room. She stared down into her cappuccino stirring the brown sugar into the froth, thankful that no-else was upstairs. Alex had ordered her drink without asking what she wanted; he remembered.

And then the small talk ceased.

"I was so glad for you when he told me he wasn't pressing charges," Janine ventured to try and get some sort of conversation going.

And she was caught off guard by the torrent that followed.

"Do you think he did that out of kindness?" Alex said. "The manipulative prick only did it to make you think he is a nice person – but you're so besotted you can't see it. I would have gladly gone down for him.

"I was in a pub last week with Nick and this girl came up to me. That was an interesting conversation – his ex girlfriend – Lucy, I think her name was. Someone told her who I was. You might want to talk to her."

"I know about her," Janine tried to intervene. "He told me she—"

"She what? Cheated on him?" And he said it with a sarcasm that she wasn't used to seeing from him. He was obviously still very angry.

"She left him because she couldn't stand his controlling personality any more. They never went anywhere unless it was to do with the band; he would never go anywhere with her unless it was with **his** friends; he would never visit her family; she gave up staying at his flat because he ignored her all night while he played his damn guitar; and weekends she spent on her own while he was rehearsing."

Janine wanted to say that he wasn't telling her anything she didn't already know. All of that sounded perfectly reasonable to her, knowing Dion's personality. He had no time for small talk, would not mix with people who bored him and was obsessed with his music – all qualities which she adored about him – but she decided against antagonising Alex further by saying any of that, so she continued staring into her coffee.

"'And I've read about the tours coming up. What are you gonna do Janine when all the eighteen-year-olds throw themselves at him eh? Think someone in their thirties can compete with that?

"Oh, and you might want to ask the asshole about the other girlfriends he sees behind your back – particularly the two in the band. The last straw for Lucy was him shagging the twins, both at the same time apparently."

Janine felt a lurch in her stomach and actually felt sick. That was not the Dion she recognised.

She tried to look impassive, as if she did not believe a word of this, but Alex picked up on her expression and she actually felt herself start to shake.

"Yes, that's your precious Dion. You think you're the only one?" And he laughed unpleasantly. "And I tell you something else about the selfish son of a bitch – he'll separate you from the kids. He's only interested in one thing so don't think it's anything to do with love. And the boys will be in the way. Mark my words, he'll make you choose, the kids or him. Maybe not now in this la la land honeymoon period, but wait and see.

"I tell you something," he said lowering his voice. "I wish I'd finished the bastard off."

"I have to go," Janine said – and spilt the coffee as she tried to replace it on the saucer with her shaking hand.

Chapter Twenty-Two

She ran down the precarious steps of the cafe to the ground floor, leaving Alex behind to fume over his coffee, and stepped outside into the late afternoon cold air.

She caught her breath sharply at the sight of Dion, standing in a shop doorway opposite the café, staring right at her and taking a long draw on a cigarette. She had never seen him with a cigarette in his hand; he was too precious about his voice. To say he looked enraged would be an understatement.

Her heart lurched and her head was immediately full of contradictions and fears. She felt as if she was the one who had been caught out cheating; she was afraid what would happen when Alex came out of the cafe in a few moments; and she was scared to tell Dion about the conversation she had just had for fear he would confirm it was the truth.

Then, she reasoned, she had nothing to hide, so she walked across the cobbled pathway to him as he continued drawing on a cigarette and blowing the smoke into the air in an exaggerated manner. He looked seriously pissed off and kept his eyes fixed on her as she walked towards him.

She didn't get chance to say anything first; Dion was straight in. He didn't need to shout, the chill in his eyes was enough.

"Do you want to say why you have arranged to have a cosy coffee with your ex without telling me?" he said. "One of my mates called into the music shop and stopped to chat. He told me he'd just seen you going into the cafe with some bloke and from the description I guessed—"

Janine decided she would give Dion a taste of his own medicine. She had watched and learned, so she looked him full in the eye with all the confidence she could muster and answered quietly in Dion-like, matter of fact way, "I just bumped into him outside the bank and he said there were things he wanted to discuss. He asked me to talk over a coffee and I didn't see the harm. I would have told you as soon as we met up. Go in and ask him if you want." And she prayed he would not accept that challenge. She kept her eyes fixed on him, standing firm, defiant, even though she felt as if she could wither under his ice blue stare.

He said nothing for at least a minute while he smoked another cigarette and looked as if he was considering her story.

He suddenly dropped his cigarette on the floor and crushed it beneath his boots, which seemed to Janine like a symbol of what was about to happen to her.

Then he caught her completely by surprise by pulling her hard and close into him and giving her the most tender, long, lingering, nicotine-tasting kiss, while his left hand blatantly gripped her bum in this public place. What Janine didn't see, as she was caught up in the moment with her eyes closed, was that Dion's eyes were wide open as he watched Alex leave the cafe – and his right arm which was wrapped behind her, was turned in a one finger salute.

She only snapped out of the moment when she heard Alex shout, "Yea, same to you, asshole. Don't say I didn't warn you, Janine."

"What did he mean, 'Same to you'?" she asked, pulling away, as Alex stormed off towards the city centre.

"I gave him the 'one finger'," he said with a self satisfied look on his face, an expression which made him look as if he enjoyed being cruel when he had to.

Janine felt used as she realised that the kiss which felt so genuine was not at all.

And, never one to let anything go, Dion was back in for the kill. "What did he want to discuss?"

Janine stuck with the pretend direct approach and her eyes bored into his, waiting for any hint of betrayal. "He told me I'm not the only girl you have; that Lucy left you because of your affairs and that you've had the twins – together."

Dion did not even blink. He grabbed her hand tightly and hauled her back to the city centre without saying a word, smoking furiously all the way. This was not their interlinked fingers way of holding hands, this was like leading a small child home where she was about to get a smack and she actually felt afraid of him.

He led her to the multi-storey car park, ignoring any, 'Hi, Dions' on the way. He was not in the mood. He opened his passenger door without saying a word and she got in – like a prisoner going to an execution. He got into the car, lit another cigarette, wound the window down in the freezing cold and drove across the city, still without saying a word.

Janine wondered whether to leap out of the car at the first opportunity. This was someone who would drive at speed straight into a brick wall if he thought it would solve a problem. And she had no idea where they were going.

Dion pulled the car into Bird Street and pulled onto a small, private car park next to a beautician's shop.

"Get out," he ordered, lighting up another cigarette.

Janine thought better of disobeying or asking any questions. She had never seen him in such a rage and she wondered if they were about to have their first ever row.

He got out of the car and hurled the cigarette onto the floor after another long drag. Dion peered into the beautician's shop window, at the ladies having their nails buffed and polished, and opened the door for Janine to walk in.

The bell tinkled pleasantly as they entered the shop but the irritating pop music was excessively loud. The young beauty therapist looked up from the glass table. As soon as she saw Dion there was an, 'Oh shit', expression on her face and she dropped the bottle of red nail varnish, which clattered and spilt all over the glass surface. The lady opposite her sat back in her chair sharply to avoid being splashed.

"Jan – this is Lucy Liar," he announced, completely unconcerned by the stares of half a dozen clients. Dion never cared about making a scene if he thought it was necessary.

Janine had never asked about Lucy. She had not wanted to know what she looked like or anything about her. After all, if he was telling the truth this was the only other person who had shared his bed and the thought made her mad with jealousy.

Lucy was extraordinarily pretty and slim. She looked stunning even in her beautician's white overall. She was only in her twenties, Janine would guess, quite small with a fake tan and wearing a lot of make-up, as you would expect with a beautician or air hostess. Her short black hair was cropped into a fashionable style, like something out of a fashion magazine and her eyebrows and lashes were immaculate.

Lucy gave Janine a look which clearly said, 'You need a good few sessions here, love'. They were total opposites in appearance and style and Janine just could not imagine Dion with her at all.

Ignoring the incredulous stares from the clients Dion said, "So, Luce – I'd like you to tell Jan who I've been sleeping with."

Janine winced, still not used to his 'no messing' approach.

"Don't worry, no repercussions, just tell her the truth."

"I don't know what you—" Lucy stuttered, looking like a rabbit caught in the headlights.

"Just tell her, it's OK. Give her names. Tell her about the twins."

There it was again. No raised voice, but chillingly menacing.

"What are you talking about?" she said.

"You met Jan's ex and told him plenty about me. Tell Jan about my affairs."

She looked completely uncomfortable and her eyes darted from one aghast client to another.

"This is not the place," she hissed.

"Fine, let's go outside for a minute," Dion insisted.

"I don't know about any affairs," she said, looking embarrassed.

"And who finished with who, Lucy?" he added.

She looked mortified, as if caught out, and the fact that it was in public only added to her anxiety.

Lucy burst out crying, but there were no tears.

"Get out," she said. "How dare you come here. I'm glad you finished with me; you did me a favour. At least Mark pays attention to me, not spending all his time with a stupid band."

And she added with pride, "He's a sales manager now – earning more than you ever did in your crappy music shop. And we're trying for a baby," she added, darting her eyes around her clients, as if that would impress everyone.

"You better stay away from the booze then, hadn't you?" Dion said triumphantly. "I'll see you around, Luce. I'll leave you to watch your paint dry."

Dion one: Rest of the world zero.

They sat in the car park for a few minutes, Dion chain smoking.

"OK. Now we'll go to the twins' house so you can speak to them," he said.

"No. No, I don't need to," Janine said. She could do without another excruciating scene, knowing full well he was telling the truth.

"What the hell did you see in her?" Janine asked. "What an air-head."

"She was pretty," he replied simply. "She came to one of our gigs, the only one she ever came to. She pretended to like rock at first, but she loved pop music, for fuck's sake. When we finished, I vowed never to waste my energy on anyone ever again unless it was someone really special, so

I concentrated on the band. I had given up any hope of finding a soul mate.

"That day, after the rehearsal, just before we drove to the hotel, do you remember how I couldn't even look at you before asking you to get in the car?"

"You ordered me to get in the car," Janine corrected and he smiled, knowing she was right.

"My head was saying, 'This is the one, this is the one', but I knew you were with someone else and I wasn't sure you felt the same way about me," he said.

The pieces of the jigsaw were beginning to fall into place. She could see why he behaved as if every second had to be filled and why he was so intolerant. But a couple of things still bothered her.

"Did you ever tell her you loved her?"

And he laughed out loud, in a better mood now. "What do you think? No, I didn't – ever – because I didn't."

"But you slept with her," Janine said. "And you stayed with her for two years."

"It only lasted that long because I hardly ever saw her. She bored me, but I'd ask her round when I felt like I needed a shag."

"That wasn't a nice thing to do," she said and Dion shrugged his shoulders.

"I know, that was another reason to get rid of her," he added. "Let her be with someone who gave a shit."

"Has she seen your tattoo?" she asked – as if it really mattered.

"No. I had that done a week after I dumped her. That was my new motto, a secret reminder to me to stay focussed and do what I want. Apart from the tattoo artist and you, no-one else has seen that tattoo – well, except me when I look at my ass in the mirror each day."

"Good," Janine said, feeling like all was well with the world.

He interlinked his fingers with her and they sat for a moment longer, staring ahead in deep thought.

"Fucking fags," Dion said as he hurled the entire packet out of the window and started up the car.

Chapter Twenty-Three

With the Garrick Theatre performance just two days away and the flat to themselves there was a little time to de-stress.

Dion and Janine were experts at that. The Alex and Lucy Liar events were put behind them and only served to enhance their resolve that nothing would stand in their way ever again. After leaving the beautician's car park they went straight home – and it was like that first night at the hotel all over again. As soon as they shut the door he took her standing up behind it. Their love making took on renewed urgency as they gradually made their way to the bedroom.

Lying utterly exhausted on the bed two hours later, Dion curled around her naked back and whispered, "You never need to worry or doubt me. Trust me, if ever I wanted an affair I would tell you, but that's never going to happen. I will always be honest with you. I can't stand lies. We are about to set off on something amazing and I need you with me."

Janine turned round and moved the hair out of his eyes and marvelled at how glorious he looked, propped up on one elbow, looking like a male porn star in the centrefold of a magazine. "I should have known better than to think for a second—but look at you, for goodness sake. And soon I have to share you with the rest of the world."

"I am going to really go for this, Jan," he said stroking her breasts. "And I'm sure there will be times when you will see the arrogant Dion Rock Star, but it's an act. I'm playing a part. Sometimes I wonder where the image ends and I begin, but this is what I've wanted my whole life. I know myself. I know what I want and that I can be uncompromising. I do recognise that I piss people off because of who I am, but actually I quite like myself for toughing things out. I hate anything left unsaid, anything left unresolved. Nothing good ever came of living a half life, living a lie – and I've seen too many people do that. I am not going to be one of those people."

Janine felt herself laugh out loud. "You are the most extraordinary person I have ever met," she told him, running her fingers down to one of his most extraordinary parts.

"I know," he answered with a shrug – and meant it. Janine was now used to his total lack of modesty and there followed a renewed, frenzied session.

The night of the Garrick Theatre gig arrived and the band members met up four hours before the start of the show for a run through with the film crew. The set was to include new songs – including the ones Dion worked on when he was 'out of it'.

The twins arrived last of all, looking stunning as usual: all legs, hair cascading over their shoulders, wearing miniskirts and high heels. Everyone was in a good mood; this was a gig to savour – a farewell on home ground before the UK tour. And for Janine, it marked the end of a teaching career and the beginning of being a professional performer.

There were hugs all round when the girls arrived and Dion, tactile as ever, went over, stood in the middle and draped an arm over each of them. 'Now there is a picture-perfect scene', Janine thought to herself. The three of them together looked as if they were made for each other and Alex's words stabbed her in the heart.

Dion looked up and caught her eye.

"Girls, come over here a minute." And he led them over to Janine, still with his arms draped over their shoulders.

"Someone told Janine I sleep with you, both at the same time," he said with a mischievous glint in his eyes as he looked directly at Janine, amused by her mortified expression.

'Oh my God', Janine thought, hardly knowing where to look. 'I should have known he wouldn't let it go. Here we go again. Straight in. No messing. Get it sorted – even on such an important night as this'.

She was horrified that the girls would be offended and this would affect the atmosphere of the whole night. She trusted him implicitly, but despite wanting to kill him at that particular moment, there was still a part of her that prepared to scrutinise their reaction.

In fact, their reaction was to pull away from him as if they had been electrocuted; it was actually quite funny to watch and was so spontaneous it would have been impossible to act.

"Oh my God, 'D'," Eva said leaping about a yard away from him. ('D' was what she always called him affectionately.) "I love you dearly, but God, no. Maybe if you let me near you with the scissors—"

169

Lou was pretending to wash herself as if the very thought made her unclean, with cries of, "Eeuw, Jesus, no. No offence, Dion, but you're just not my type."

There was no more to be said. Dion simply fixed his eyes on Janine, smiled his mischievous smile, mouthed, 'See'? with a gesture of his arms and leapt from the floor onto the stage to help set up the equipment.

Janine turned to the twins; she could tell them apart easily now, though it had taken her a while. "Eva, I'm sorry, that was so embarrassing," she said. "I could kill him sometimes."

"It's OK," Eva replied. "Actually we get that all the time. We both get sick of saying, 'HE'S NOT MY TYPE'. No offence, Janine, but you should get him to do something about all that hair."

Lou was now pretending to stick her fingers down her throat and throw up.

"Sorry, Janine," she said as she caught her eye. "We love him, but Jesus, Mary, mother of God—"

Typical Dion. He could have let it go, but no – situation sorted.

With the sound check done and everyone more or less happy with the set-up, the band made their way to the dressing rooms. Dion took an electric guitar with him for some last-minute practice. This was a first tonight; as well as lead vocals he would be playing guitar on three of the songs, the ones he wrote while in his 'other place'. Although not as accomplished as the other musicians he was good enough to carry it off – and what he lacked in expertise he could more than disguise by following the others, standing in front of them, making it look as if they were studying each other intently on stage and enjoying the moment - and posing rock god style with guitar slung around him.

Janine stood on a chair and took a sneak peek through the high window. The crowds were already queued up around the block and she felt a mixture of fear and excitement. Dion had no such fear; she never once saw him with pre show nerves. She envied his confidence and the way he was able to laugh and chat with everyone over a pint, almost up to the point where they were about to go on stage. He had done the homework; he was well rehearsed. What was there to worry about? That was his view.

Once Janine was in her black and red dress (she had now ordered several which were similar, but with subtle differences) she was in her role. Now she was not Dion's girlfriend, she was a performer in her own right. Here we go.

The intro tape sounded, the drumming so loud that the audience could feel it in their ribcage and the roar of the crowd was deafening.

Unlike the Mistress set, the Son of Gabriel songs included several which were on the theme of love lost or found, but all with a hard-ass message, like, it's over, you bitch; I'm going to take you from your other half; or you wear me out at night.

The first song, *Marathon Man'* a real belter, was one such song – and it had nothing to do with running whatsoever—

It was one of those rare nights when everything came together. At the end of *Marathon Man* the band launched straight into their second song, *Love Me Tonight* ('love' maybe having not much to do with it) then paused for the first time for applause. This was the audience's first chance to express their appreciation. They had all read about Dion's attack, many had supported the fundraisers and they all shared a pride that their local band was going on to greater things. There was a sense that they were there that night to experience something special.

At the end of the second song it was as if there was a wave of affection coming from the crowd. All the seats had been removed and apart from those on the balcony, most of the audience was standing on the flat floor.

The applause, cheers and the roar from the crowd went on and on, gradually giving way to a chant, which started in a small group at the front of the stage, then travelled like a Mexican wave throughout the audience. They were chanting, 'Di-on, Di-on, Di-on', over and over.

Dion raised his hand as if to say, 'Thanks, but enough now', but the chant carried on and became louder.

'Di-on, Di-on, Di-on'. He gestured up and down with his hands as if to quieten things down, but the crowd was having none of it. This was way out of his comfort zone; normally when he commanded, people obeyed, on stage and off.

Then the chanting gave way to applause, a standing ovation just for Dion. Janine and the band turned towards him, joining the audience in their tribute.

Janine watched as his rock star composure started to slip.

Totally overwhelmed by the reaction of the fans (who were mostly wearing Rock For Dion T shirts) and touched by the love of his band, he stood there and actually cried. With every fibre of her being Janine wanted to wrap her arms around him and comfort him as he openly sobbed in the spotlight. But this was not her boyfriend; this was Dion Rock Star. The sight of him looking so vulnerable made her crumble too and she broke her heart openly on stage, as all the memories of months in the hospital flooded back. That set the twins off and everyone on stage was a mess.

All this, and the band had only performed two songs of the set.

Dion tried again to quieten the crowd and eventually they stood silent in anticipation, waiting for him to speak.

"Thank you," he said in the silence, his voice breaking with emotion. "God, what a bunch of bastards you are. Look what you've done to me." And the audience laughed, then fell silent again in anticipation.

"Wow." He paused. "It's been quite a journey and I'm here thanks to you (and he indicated to the crowd and the band)." There were more cheers from the crowd.

"I'd like to thank the band for waiting for me to recover - and I'd like to thank you, Jan," he said, turning to her, "for spending months at the hospital and never giving up on me." (Cheers).

He wiped the tears away, then took a deep breath, completely unashamed of having laid himself bare in front of a crowd of mostly burly rock guys.

"Now stop with the fucking man-love and let's rock."

He picked up a guitar, slung it defiantly round his neck and his composure was instantly back. "This is one I wrote while I was away with the fairies in hospital," he said and launched into a blistering riff which crashed into the walls of the theatre.

The band had not arranged any special effects; they knew the Mistress magic would take care of that; and Dion was absolutely of the opinion that any phenomena would only enhance the performance in a good way. And he was right, of course, as usual.

There were mysterious sparkles on the stage which drew visible gasps from the theatre staff, who considered running for the fire extinguishers; there were holograms and silhouettes; and random messages projected onto the walls – always all in keeping with the songs.

The band members had come to terms with such things and resolved not to question them, but trust in Dion when he said everything would be fine and this was how it was meant to be.

The whole night was a triumph. It included the anthem *Magic of Rock*, which gave the audience another opportunity to take over; Janine's *When You Wake*, and ended with another 'written while I was out of it' song called *Thank You For the Ride* featuring Dion on guitar. Although the lyrics were open to interpretation, he said it was about a girl who was hitch-hiking and got picked up by a guy.

Leaving the stage with chants of 'Di-on' still ringing in their ears the band made their way to the dressing rooms fit to drop.

Janine kept her eyes fixed on Dion to make sure he was OK. This was meant to have been a 'try out' gig to see if he was well enough to go on tour. But typically, he had not eased himself in gently; he had given it his all and he was exhausted.

They declined an after show party and she drove him home at midnight, when he went straight to bed without a word and was asleep as soon as his head hit the pillow. When Janine got up about ten a.m. he was still sleeping soundly. By twelve noon she was getting concerned so she took him a coffee and tried to wake him. He opened his eyes sleepily.

"You OK?" she said moving a random wave of hair out of eyes, as she often did. "Wasn't last night's gig amazing?"

"I have something I need to tell you," he whispered sleepily. And the urgency in the way he said it made her blood run cold.

Chapter Twenty-Four

Dion sat up in bed and drank his coffee which slowly brought him back to reality.

"I need a piss," he announced and went to the bathroom, totally naked. The central heating had gone off so he quickly snuggled back into bed, shivering under the duvet.

"It's Saturday morning; get back into bed," he said.

"Dion, it would be nice if sometimes you said 'please' instead of ordering me about," she answered, but was already removing her jeans and T shirt anyway.

"And the rest," he said looking her up and down – without saying, 'please'. She did as she was told and snuggled next to him, enjoying the feel and smell of his skin and her anxiety melted away.

"What was it you wanted to say?" she asked, her hand sliding around his waist.

He was lying on his side facing Janine, enjoying the comfort of the pillow and hoping it would cushion his words. But there was no sugar-coating this one.

Janine was on her side too looking into eyes just inches away and desperate for a clue. She could sense him struggling to find the right words. 'Most unlike him', she thought. 'Usually he just dives straight in'. And that made her feel really uneasy.

"You're not going to like this," he said quietly, interlinking his fingers into hers and kissing the back of her hand.

"Dion, you're killing me. Just tell me."

"Do you remember when we were in the hospital and you were asking me questions about where I said I had been? Do you remember I said I would tell you when I was ready and when the time is right? And I said I would wait until we were lying on the pillows in our own bed?

She gave a slight nod and waited.

He gave an outward sigh, blowing hard, as if to prepare her.

"Jan, the time is right to tell you now. We pulled off the gig last night – and yes, it was amazing. I'm knackered, but we proved I am fit enough for the tour. We are about to set off on a UK tour, then Europe, then America and live the dream. And I need to tell you what I have to say while the kids are away for the weekend. You are going to need this weekend for yourself."

Janine felt she could hardly breathe and she could hear her heat thumping in her ears. What could be so bad that she would need a weekend without the kids to hear? Was he having affairs despite all the assurances he had given her? Were his words all an elaborate charade? Was Alex right?

"I want you to know I love you so much," he whispered, looking at her with those captivating blue eyes, clearly full of love, but also of merciless directness.

"So what can be so important?" she whispered. "We have everything, we are going places and I adore you."

"You will only have me for another six years."

That did just not compute. The brain just would not take that in. But somehow, her words were coming out automatically.

"What do you mean, six years? What are you talking about?"

And he breathed in and blew out his warm breath onto her hand.

"What are you saying? Oh, my God, are you telling me you have some sort of illness? That's it, isn't it? Oh, dear God, you've slept for nearly twelve hours. How can I have been so stupid to think you were just tired?"

"Jan – that's not it. I'm not ill, I'm fine. I have never been happier. I am just telling you that I will not be reaching forty."

"But, what are you on about? What do you mean, you will not be reaching forty?"

"Because I choose not to," he said, which slammed into her chest and took her breath away. She could feel her pulse racing.

"What on earth are you saying? That you are going to kill yourself and leave me before you are forty?"

And his silence spoke volumes.

"Jan." He took both of her hands and held them to his lips, kissing them tenderly.

"I have always known I will not see forty, but more importantly, I don't want to be forty. I don't want to be that person who grows old, who has greying hair and wrinkles, who puts on weight, who has aches and pains – knowing things can only get worse. I want to always be the person I am now."

Janine's voice was rising now and there was a touch of hysteria creeping in. She hardly even recognised the voice that came out of her.

"But no-one wants that. What makes you so different?" And even as she said it, she knew that he was different – and that thought terrified her.

"Please don't tell me you have already worked out a way to kill yourself."

"There's more that I need to tell you," he added, now holding her hands tightly so she could not move out of the bed. "And you are going to freak."

He paused to breathe hard.

"I told you when I was in a coma that I went somewhere."

Janine was so desperate to get him out of this conversation that she continued to interrupt.

"But that wasn't real. Lots of people have said they see things when they were in a coma. It isn't true. It's just your brain playing tricks."

"Jan. I wrote songs while I was there. The only way I can describe it is – you know when you talk to people who are really depressed and they say they are in 'a dark place'? Well I really was in a place – only it wasn't dark; it was timeless with the essence of creative people. It's hard to explain."

She was trying to pull away now, horrified by what she was hearing and upset beyond words.

"I'm not talking about a kind of heaven," he said, putting his arm around her waist and pulling him to her. "But it was somewhere real."

Janine's tears now started to flow, soaking the pillow and her hair and she seriously wondered whether Dion needed some kind of therapy. But his next words ripped her heart out and stamped on it.

"Jan, I saw how it will end. I will be thirty-nine – and it will be beautiful."

"Dion, stop," she said struggling to breathe at all. And she put her fingers over his lips as if that would stop him, unable to bear to listen to any more.

He pulled her tightly into him, nuzzled into her hair and whispered in her ear, "And you will be with me. You're coming with me."

"What?" she screamed, wrenching herself away from him, with Alex's words echoing in her head: 'Mark my words, he will make you choose. It will be the kids or him'.

She was out of the bed now, screaming at him like something demented.

"You mad, selfish, selfish bastard. How can you say this to me? You are asking me to enter some kind of fucking suicide pact?"

She had always known he was self-obsessed and selfish but this was something else.

"I have two kids, you crazy bastard. I'll never leave my kids for you or anyone else."

She collapsed onto the floor sobbing uncontrollably. Dion got out of the bed and held her to him, rocking her like a child until she quietened down, exhausted. He pulled the duvet off the bed and wrapped it round them to keep them warm.

"Dion, we've been together for less than a year," she said through her tears. "And in that time you've made me fall hopelessly in love with you. And for what? To tell me you would have me die with you and leave my kids behind? Are you insane?"

"But it's not a suicide pact, Jan," he said, his matter of fact style now seriously annoying her. "I saw it. We will go together. And Jan, I've worked it out. You won't be leaving your kids. They won't be kids. They will be eighteen and twenty-one by then. You are coming with me."

Chapter Twenty-Five

Janine spent the next few hours in a state of panic, putting the wrong things into the wrong cupboards in the kitchen, loading stuff into the washing machine that didn't belong in there, putting the washing powder in the fridge – and feeling utterly demented. She could not think straight at all and his words were going round and round in her head.

After such a monumental announcement she expected Dion to be attentive towards her, to talk about his bombshell, to comfort her – but she found herself enraged simply because he was acting perfectly normal.

He dealt with phone calls, talking about travel plans for the tour; phoned his mum in Spain and told her everything was 'fine'; played his records; picked up his guitar; took a shower; and offered to make cheese on toast.

Janine seriously wanted to bash that guitar over his head and push the toast into his face.

Every now and then he would come up behind her, put his arms round her waist and pull her to him. She could feel he was aroused, but pulled away as he put his hands down the front of her jeans.

"Don't – touch – me," she said and turned to him with a face like thunder.

He went to say something but with uncharacteristic bravery she added, "Shut up. Don't-even-talk-to me."

She never stood up to him; she never usually had cause to, she reasoned; even when he was being demanding she excused his behaviour as 'that's just him'; and he knew he could usually bring her round simply by making her look into his eyes and saying something irreverent, witty or endearing.

But today her world had fallen apart.

"I need to get out of the flat," she said. "I need some air or I will go crazy."

Dion never liked her to be out of his sight and she knew that.

"I need to be on my own for a while. You might be able to carry on as normal, but I'm not being a part of this."

And she picked up her car keys, avoided his eyes and left with no idea where she was going or for how long. She bashed her hands up and down on the steering wheel in temper and screamed out loud before starting up the car, then drove off tearfully without looking back. Where to go in a time of crisis?

Janine pulled into Cathedral Close and was relieved to see it was quiet on this cold winter's day. She abandoned the car, parking it in an unauthorised spot, and made her way inside the cathedral where she felt some kind of peace.

She sat near the front in one of the pews and cried softly. The word 'desperate' did not even come close to how she felt so she prayed, hoping no visitors would notice her. "Please, if there is a God give me something to cling on to," she said, trying to project her thoughts into the very fabric of the building. "Make him see he is talking nonsense. Take away all these ideas he has in his head. You gave him to me – please don't take him away after such a short time." And she repeated her plea over and over.

But this was Dion – and her heart chilled at the thought that he never changed his mind, never compromised, never discussed, never saw another point of view. He always trusted his own instincts and she knew deep down that no amount of reasoning or pleading would persuade him. Dion did what Dion wanted. She sat for at least an hour, pleading into the universe in the belief that at least this could do no harm. A couple of people were glancing over to her and she started to feel uneasy and a little stupid, so she got up to leave.

Dion was standing against the back wall.

Today the sun was not shining, he was dressed all in black and even his hair could not make him look like an angel.

"I followed you - obviously," he said as she walked past him without speaking or even looking at him.

She was already resigned to his plan. She would have six years and that would be it. All she could do was try to make the most of them and hope that he would change his mind. She figured he had such a huge ego that once he had all the adulation he desired, he was not going to give that up lightly.

If she was wrong, however he chose to do it, he would be doing it alone - of that she was sure.

Chapter Twenty-Six

They had driven back to their flat in separate cars. Even that had felt significant that day.

Once inside, and with Dion unusually quiet, she was the one who tried to lay down the law. He didn't tell her, of course, but when she had walked out of the flat earlier he was terrified she was leaving him.

She was making coffee in the kitchen when he walked in and stood leant against the worktops watching her.

"I have a few things to say, then I am never going to say them again, do you understand?" Janine said, doing her best to chill him with her gaze and failing miserably.

He nodded, trying not to look amused at her taking a stand.

"One: I think you're ridiculous.

"Two: are you saying that when you are forty you are going to look so different from when you are thirty-nine and thre hundred and sixty-four days old?"

"I don't want to be one of those people who 'look good for forty'," Dion answered.

"Shut up. I'm talking for once," Janine snapped.

And he looked down to hide his smile. She had asked a question after all; he had only answered.

"Three: what about your mum and dad?"

"Do you want me to reply now?" he said sarcastically.

"Yes," she said, trying to sound definite, but realising he was already getting the upper hand.

But she was well caught off guard by his answer.

"They know. I told them I would not be forty. That's why they moved to Spain. Mum said she would rather leave me than the other way round. She couldn't bear it, she got it into her head that I could do it at any time, so they left. When they had the call from the hospital they thought at first—"

Janine had the incredulous look back on her face.

"You really are the most selfish person I have ever met. I can't believe – well – yes I can actually – knowing you. I feel so sorry for your lovely parents."

Then, struggling to remember where she had got to Janine added, "Number four. (Dion smirked at her trying to keep her thoughts on track and be assertive at the same time) Stop smirking, you inconsiderate bastard."

"Was that number four, or were you just having a go at me?" he said.

She took a deep breath and tried again, determined not to let him get the better of her for once.

"Number four: when is this supposed to happen? When you are thirty-nine and one day old, thirty-nine and three hundred and sixty-four days old or what?"

"I don't know exactly, but I'll know when the time is right and I will tell you," he said, taking back control of the conversation.

"Number five: you have never had kids of your own. If you had, you would know that they are always your kids – however old they are."

Dion looked unmoved. She waited for a response, but none came, and that intense look was enough to take her off guard so she moved on.

"Number six: you said you saw how it will end, but you never described it to me. You can't just say that and leave it in mid-air. What do you mean, you will just 'go'? How will you 'go'?

"I'll tell you when it's time. You'll see for yourself," he said with unflinching conviction. "You'll freak if I tell you beforehand."

She fixed her best glare at him, not satisfied with the answer, but realising she would get no more.

"Number seven: when you 'go' what do you want to happen to your dead body?"

"Do you think I would leave this behind to deteriorate?" he said, striking a rock star pose with imaginary guitar and flouncing his hair.

"Seriously," Janine tried again, getting angrier by the minute (little realising he was serious), "If there was no body, you moron, where would people say you were?"

"That's a separate question, so that must be number eight," he said, looking bored now.

Janine did not react, trying to give him a taste of his own medicine.

"There would be conspiracy theories, Jan. People would take photos for years to come all over the world of some poor, old, fat, bald man and claim it was me, just like they do with Elvis. They'd say the pressure of fame got too much for me so I just took off somewhere in disguise, etcetera."

"You really have thought of everything haven't you, you smart arse?" she replied, "And yes, (trying her hand at sarcasm) I realise that's another question. Don't bother answering."

"Number eight," Janine said decisively (and he rolled his eyes to the heavens as if to say 'Have we nearly finished'?) "Whatever you choose to do, you will do it on your own. I will not leave my kids. Is that clear?"

"Is there a number nine?" he said.

She realised he was taking the piss. He always knew how to push the buttons and was the master of sarcasm. She had witnessed him demolish other people like this so many times.

"Just fuck off," she said, feeling drained. And it occurred to her that it must be exhausting being Dion. Her feeble effort was nothing to how he spoke to people all the time.

Janine had another attempt at sorting out the washing - while Dion did fuck off – and stood in the back garden, chain smoking.

Chapter Twenty-Seven

Lichfield Rock Band Launch Charity,
  by Pat Leasowe.

Local rock band Son of Gabriel launched a new charity in the city this week.

The charity, called Rock For Dion, will fund rehearsal time and recording sessions at local venues and studios for aspiring young rock bands.

It is the brainchild of lead singer/guitarist Dion Freeman, who said he wished to put something back into the industry which has given him so much.

Mr Freeman, aged thirty-three, from Burntwood, said the gesture is also to thank the many fans who donated to his Rock For Dion fund, which paid for private intensive physio sessions as he recovered from an attack in the city which happened in June. Mr Freeman suffered head injuries and broken ribs in the unprovoked incident which took place at the rear of the city's Arts Centre and was in a coma for three and a half months.

He said, 'Fans raised so much money that there is still a sizeable amount left. I have been thinking about how best to use the money and how I can continue to generate more income for the project.

'We will be holding bucket collections at all future gigs, with every penny raised going into the fund. We will also be pleased to accept any donations.

'Bands who are struggling to meet the costs of rehearsal rooms and studios can send a demo tape and apply for grant aid. Those whose music shows potential will be awarded a grant to cover ongoing costs.

'My aim is also to support local recording studios and venues – particularly the Arts Centre which I understand was earmarked for closure'.

Son of Gabriel will be setting off for a UK tour next month after Friday's triumphant launch at Lichfield's Garrick Theatre where their debut album was filmed. The band, which is renowned for its unique special effects, is already booked to headline in stadiums across Europe.

Lichfield District Council chairman Councillor Mrs Dorothy Huff said: 'This is a welcome gesture from Mr Freeman. What a fine young man. Having such a high profile band is a real feather in the cap for our great city'.

Cllr Huff confirmed there are now no current plans to close the Arts Centre.

Application forms for grant aid are available from local music shops and our newspaper office. Donations payable to 'Rock for Dion Fund' will also be accepted there.

The article carried a new picture of Dion in rock star pose, alongside a photo of Cllr Huff who looked as if she had swallowed a wasp.

Typically, Dion had mentioned nothing about his idea to Janine, who was surprised to read the front page story when the paper dropped through their letterbox.

She could imagine that Greyman had declined to write such a positive story and passed it on to another reporter.

"I just thought I'd whack out a press release," Dion said dismissively as he sat on the bed strumming his guitar. "I just didn't know what else to do with the cash."

"I think it's a great idea, what a lovely thing to do," she said kissing the top of his head. But there was a small part of her which wondered whether the charity wasn't more to do with keeping Dion's name in the public consciousness.

"I can be nice," he said – without a trace of sincerity.

The UK tour was to take six months and Janine was relieved that, with some juggling and the help of her family and ex husband, she could sort out childcare, return home regularly and the kids could join the tour during school holidays. They would have a tutor for the European leg of the tour, as per Dion's instructions. He had no problem with taking the kids; he enjoyed their company, made sure they behaved and looked forward to 'down time' with them. When he wasn't working he was still fun to be around, always up for mischief and a real party animal.

The performance dates had been spread out to allow time to recover, the longest run without a break being three nights. Miles had organised the venues at major cities meticulously after Dion had a major strop and threatened to pull out of the tour. He said he was not prepared to dart up and down the country without any logical pattern geographically. He also demanded a tour bus for the band and crew. As the natural leader, the band left all such negotiations to him; and anyway it was easier that way because he generally got what he wanted, did know best and there was zero chance of anyone trying to persuade him otherwise. If someone did make a suggestion which he thought was genuinely useful he would embrace it and show his appreciation with enthusiasm, but that wasn't often as he had usually thought of everything anyway – even down to the lighting, sound, publicity and logistics. As far as effects were concerned, his attitude was to trust his instincts that such things were already being taken care of, going on past experiences, and any ideas he had were mere 'additions' to enhance the show.

Whatever he could be accused of, it could never be said that he was lazy. He was professional to a fault, always word-perfect, well-rehearsed, punctual, gave one hundred per cent on stage to the point of exhaustion at every show and never, ever missed a concert.

On the downside he demanded exactly the same of every member of the band and crew. Anything less than perfection resulted in scathing criticism and exhausting re-runs.

Technicians and the press in towns across the UK loathed him. Whereas most people setting off on their first high profile tour may have trodden carefully to find their feet, Dion was a monster from day one.

He never raised his voice, never had to; the tone, the sarcasm and the look would be enough. Janine was used to it by now, but there were many who were reduced to tears or simply refused to work with him. As she witnessed him tear some minion apart she would often leave the scene, finding it too painful to watch.

His worst tantrums were reserved for video recording sessions which turned into a nightmare for all concerned; but many aspects of being in a band infuriated him.

"Can you find me a technician who knows what they are doing?" he would ask over the microphone during sound checks, usually followed by, "Now."

"Lights man, I only have two retinas and I'm going to need them for the rest of the tour."

"Do you have any original questions?" he would ask reporters, then get up and leave.

One young male reporter who dared to criticise Dion's image ended up ripped apart in front of his colleagues by a savage attack about his spots, greasy hair and cheap chain store clothing.

TV presenters also had their share. "Perhaps if you did your research—" he would start if they asked questions he felt they should know the answers to.

"What do you call this, the caravan suite?" he asked one hotel manager who had to move heaven and earth to arrange better accommodation.

"I'm not eating this shit. Do you want to take it home for your dog?" he said to some hapless chef.

"No, I won't be posing like that, it'll look fucking ridiculous," to a photographer.

And on and on.

Such was his reputation that one poor female reporter from a local paper, on being told she was to interview him, had to walk round a park for an hour beforehand, breathing deeply to avoid a panic attack.

The interview was to be with other journalists in a pub called the Stumble Inn, specially cordoned off for the occasion. Dion turned up exactly on time, wearing ordinary jeans and T shirt but looking extraordinary. He sat down and the assembled reporters stood around uncomfortably, too scared to take any of the seats near him. The reporter who was still trying to keep her panic attack at bay momentarily felt sorry for him sitting alone, surrounded by empty seats, so she took a deep breath, plonked herself right next to him, introduced herself and welcomed him to the town.

She was so nervous she launched into a string of questions, talked too fast and was totally thrown by his piercing blue eyes which stared in amusement at her. But he liked people with courage and he gave her an amazing interview, much to the annoyance of all the other reporters who remained frozen out by his glare. And he posed good-naturedly with her for a photo which she framed and kept long after the occasion.

But such events were rare; usually someone somewhere came in for it. And to be fair, if he complained he was usually justified, it was just that no-one else would have had the balls to say it.

Only the regular stage hands seem to escape his wrath, mostly because they worked hard, he liked them as individuals, joked around with them on the tour bus and many of them were his mates. But even they could not rely on friendship to save them if they tried to take advantage. And drug use of any kind on tour was an absolute instant sackable offence.

When there was time to relax in between concerts Dion and Janine would leave the hotel and visit local places, usually causing mayhem wherever they went because they were so recognisable by now. Janine hated it, but Dion relished all the attention, and the chaos their appearance caused amused him.

Back in Lichfield Cllr Dorothy Huff picked up her post from the little basket behind the letterbox in the hallway. "Oh, how nice, dear," she said to her husband. "Someone has sent me a postcard." It was a really pretty postcard of a seaside town, very quaint and beautiful. It read:

Hi Cllr Huff
Having a lovely time. Saw the newspaper article. Glad to hear you now think I am a fine young man.
Thought you looked a bit uptight on your photo.
If you ever fancy a fuck give me a call.
Love Dion

But there were others, all written during bored moments in some hotel somewhere.

Hi Alex
Thank you to you and your mate for trying to smash my head in.
Thanks to you the publicity helped to fast-track my inevitable rise to stardom.
Oh – and thanks for your girlfriend. Having plenty of sun, sea and sex.
Glad you're not here.
Dion

Hi Greyman
Playing sell-out tours. Booked up solid for the next six years abroad.

Very rich. Thanks for all your support. No such thing as bad publicity.
Enjoy smallsville and being a big fish in a little pond.
Happy nine till five.
Dion

He never told Janine about the postcards but often smiled to himself as he pictured their reaction.

When they returned home for a break after a few months he worked on new ideas for the Rock for Dion fund. Money was pouring in faster than it was going out so he decided to extend his idea and help aspiring bands across the UK. He set up an office in Lichfield where the fund could be co-ordinated by paid staff, specially selected by him, of course. He gave the job of listening to all the demo tapes to a couple of guys from one of his former bands who he had remained in contact with and trusted their opinion. Actually the fund could now run without Dion – and he was OK with that because he had enough to do, though he checked in on things from time to time.

It was also clear they were going to have to live elsewhere as life was becoming increasingly difficult at their flat. Fans had started to camp outside and Dion was getting seriously pissed off and over protective about his precious car. Diva he may have been but he took home life seriously, glad to have Janine to himself and to have some normality for a while. And since he could hardly walk around Lichfield any more to meet his old boss or mates, he figured he needed somewhere where they could come to him.

"I've bought a house," he announced to Janine as she sat reading the paper, trying to catch up on local news.

"What? What do you mean, 'I've bought a house'?"

"Well, we said we would need to move – and I just saw this perfect house advertised – so I bought it cash – and when the kids are older they can have it."

"What?" (This was a word she found herself using often in exasperated tone.) "Why would you do that? Why would you just go ahead, as usual feet first, and do such a thing without consulting me? What if I don't like it? What if the kids won't want it? Where the hell is it?

"I'll try and answer your questions in order. I always do stuff without asking you; you will like it and so will the kids. It's in Cannock Wood, a really nice big Georgian style house once owned by the local MP; it has large gardens surrounded by high walls; six bedrooms; and plenty of space for a recording studio.

"And I thought we could have a dog."

So that was that. Within two months they had moved in – and so had the dog.

Chapter Twenty-Eight

The European tour kicked off the following year and Dion was thrilled that his parents would be attending one of the gigs in Barcelona.

Janine was also looking forward to meeting them again and keen for his mum to see that he was in his element and very happy.

The tour started in France and after the first three nights the band had a few days to relax in a luxury hotel in Cannes. With his mates keeping constantly in touch with him, Dion often received news about home, so while sunning himself on the balcony he penned another postcard.

Hi Lucy Liar

Congratulations on persuading Mark to get you pregnant.

Sorry to hear he's left you already. Hope the benefits payments will be enough to survive on when you leave work.

Just bought a massive and expensive Georgian house in very posh Cannock Wood.

Sending this postcard to you from a luxury suite in Cannes. Hope you like the photo. It's in France if you don't know – oh and you don't pronounce the 's' in Cannes.

Dion

This time Lucy cried real tears. Janine didn't get to hear about that postcard either.

Janine was also enjoying an idle moment in the hotel leafing through an English magazine. There was an article about signs of the zodiac which intrigued her. Dion was an Aquarian so she read the section about his personality traits.

Aquarius men are intelligent, social, independent, excellent communicators, frank, imaginative, truthful, just, curious, affectionate, unpredictable, stubborn, obstinate and inflexible.

Independent, a little overwhelming, genius with thoughts and new ideas.

Inventive and original, churning out amazing and creative solutions.

Offbeat and eccentric. Won't be fenced in; values liberty above all else.

Loves travel, a trailblazer not a follower. Unusual and creative.

Non-conformist about his wardrobe, career and lifestyle.

Will see through anything he starts to its bitter end.

Gregarious, seems to know everyone, but not everyone understands him.

His feelings are often hidden and his reactions complex.

Uses prodding questions and indecipherable actions.

Intriguing, has a flirty charm.

Loves deeply and sincerely and would give his life for his other half in an instant.

An inferno of passion between the sheets. Nothing is too provocative or challenging in the bedroom, or more often, out of it.

Attracted to intelligence; his partner has to be someone who understands his grand designs for life and humanity.

Needs absolute freedom, wants his own space.

Happy to share his life with a smart, self-reliant partner who supports his need for autonomy.

Interesting to be around and has a large circle of friends.

A romantic, dedicated partner.

Highly unpredictable, can rationalize all options and then make a choice you'd least expect.

A sound negotiator; extremely difficult person to fool in business matters.

Takes the occasional well planned risk.

If he has a contract to sign he'll read the fine print first.

Dresses to please himself, not those around him.

Self-assured and outgoing

A confusing companion at times.

Loyal and values true friendship.

Unemotional, or at least not obviously so. Needs communication to be intimate in his relationships.

Enjoys holding hands. Will give unconditional love to the right partner.

Not interested in bargain hunting.

If he can keep his contradictory nature in check and be flexible with employees, he would make a good leader.

Had they met him? She laughed out loud then cut out the article to keep. But one of the phrases lingered in her head for hours afterwards:

Loves deeply and sincerely and would give his life for his other half in an instant.

If he would give his life for her then surely he would agree to live for her?

Since the devastating 'pillow talk' on that Saturday morning she had always had fear in the back of her mind; but the matter had never been discussed since, so she took that as a positive sign. After all, he was living the dream; anyone could see that.

Janine was enjoying having the kids with her; Dion was happy with the education they were receiving from their tutor and from studying Europe. His view was that they would learn so much more from visiting the countries than reading about them in a school room.

The boys loved their new life – apart from missing the dog, a young, fat, black mongrel which Dion christened Rolo. Janine's brother and sister, who regarded Dion as slightly mad, were given the task of taking it in turns caring for the dog and the house while they were away.

As they performed at venues across Europe the 'stage effects' seemed to be getting more phenomenal with each performance and it was becoming increasingly difficult to explain them away as 'illusions'. Some of the effects had started to hit the headlines.

The sparkly effect, which appeared randomly on stage most nights were becoming ever more spectacular. Janine had added the colour red to her blonde locks – and the mix of colours looked amazing under the stage lights.

Dion Monster continued, but he was now also Dion Sex God.

He encouraged the fans with his suggestive moves. He went out on a catwalk, getting closer to the audience where they could just about touch when he teased.

The walk back to dressing room each night was a nightmare but Dion seemed to enjoy the screams and adulation. He allowed them to touch, throw their arms around him and kiss him – and he responded. He signed various parts of their bodies or underwear; and some of the girls were absolutely gorgeous.

This is exactly what Alex had warned Janine about that day at the cafe. It had not been as much of an issue in the UK, but the Europeans were much less inhibited – but what did take her by surprise was his acceptance of male attention.

And there were double standards going on. If she or the twins received any male attention the security guys were on them like a ton of bricks and they were hurled out of the venue unceremoniously – as instructed by Dion.

When she brought up the subject with him it was dismissed outright as, "I'm Dion Rock Star. I warned you that you would see these things. I'm doing my job; this is what the girls and some guys want. Anyway, none of them ever gets as far as inside the dressing room or further than a kiss. You're the only one who goes to bed with me. How lucky are you?"

And she couldn't argue with that.

He didn't even try to tone down his act when his parents joined them for the Barcelona gig later in the tour.

Janine cringed as his mum watched his usual antics, but was surprised to see her laughing.

Speaking the following afternoon in his mum's hotel room, Janine felt she should say something.

"He never goes any further than teasing and flirting, you know," she said. "I just thought I should let you know."

"I understand it's all playing the part," she said. "I think it's funny. It's just lovely to see him so happy."

They spent the afternoon chatting and sharing stories, Janine laughing as his mum told her about the trouble he got into at high school: for refusing to cut his hair; telling the teachers they were rubbish; insisting on taking his guitar to school; punching one lad who called him 'a girl'; bunking off from lessons he found boring; and refusing to attend a careers meeting, saying, 'I already know what I want to do'. It sounded so familiar.

Neither of them spoke about the obvious and neither of them talked about his upcoming 35th birthday – which, like all of his birthdays, he had flatly refused to celebrate in any way other than by having drinks with the band and crew.

The following afternoon was another day off, but rather than battle their way through fans everyone stayed in the hotel, chilling out and catching up on movies.

Dion was in a good mood, enjoying down time with Janine and the boys and teasing her mercilessly. Janine was ironing her kids' clothes when Dion indicated to the boys to keep quiet as he crept up behind her, slipped his arms around her waist and hugged her tight, with his fingers interlocked in front of her.

"Dion, for goodness sake, let go, I'm trying to—"

But he kissed the back of her neck and the boys laughed.

"Get off me, you fool. Go and write songs or something."

"Say you love me three times and I'll let you go."

She struggled, irritated, but he held her tight.

"I love you three times," she said.

"Say it," he insisted.

"It," Janine said struggling harder.

"Then, feeling his grip tighten further on her she added, "Oh for f— I love you, now let me go. I can't breathe."

"Three times," Dion said playfully.

The boys loved it when they messed about like this and laughed at their mum trying to prise his hands off her and stamp on his feet to get free. But he was able to step backwards and still hold her tight, which annoyed the hell out of her.

Janine hated to give in to him, because that's what everyone always did, so she tried bargaining instead.

"OK, if I say 'I love you' three times will you let go of me then make me a coffee?"

"Deal."

"I love you, I love you, I love you. Now fuck off."

So he let go and made the coffee.

There were breaks in the tour when they could go home and they were really happy times. Dion loved messing about in the garden with the boys and Rolo; his former boss and Janine's family would come and stay; and there would be time set aside for work in the studio.

But then it was back to Europe and Dion would be thirty-six by the end of the tour.

Chapter Twenty-Nine

The tour marched on with more travel, more countries and more fun.

Not once did Dion moan about going back on the road. The band's record sales were constantly riding high in the rock charts and it seemed as if the demand for their concerts was insatiable.

Dion instructed everyone to enjoy it while it lasted. He was only too well aware of the many bands which had foundered because of drug use, fallen from grace, split up because of arguments or became yesterday's news as new ones came along.

Sometimes Miles would join the band for parts of the tour, keen to keep an eye on goings on – particularly on the phenomena front. After all, if it couldn't be explained away as special effects he felt he would have a problem on his hands. But he had other reasons to spend time with them, Dion and Janine in particular.

The fact that Dion was usually obnoxious to those he felt were being inefficient did not bother Miles; it actually amused him. He and Dion were similar in some respects: they were both no-nonsense people, liked fun and they got on well. Miles also liked Janine and would spend hours on the tour bus enthralling her kids with card games and simple magic tricks to while away the time.

The boys would often come running to the back of the bus in excitement, talking about some awesome trick Miles had done.

The sound of the bus's engine droned on and on, creating a hypnotic effect. It was getting towards the end of the tour and they had just performed three nights in a row so everyone was tired - even the boys, who went to their 'bus bunks' as they called them, without being told.

Dion, Janine and Miles sat in an area which had been laid out like a small lounge, enjoying a late drink with their feet up, lulled by the sound of the tyres on the tarmac. They were expecting an appraisal of how the tour and record sales were going from Miles, but Janine was the first to speak, after checking on the boys.

"They love your card games," she said. "They say you are really good. Show us a couple of tricks."

Miles took a pack of cards from his pocket and placed them on the table.

"You sure you're ready for this?" he mocked as he removed a coin from behind his ear.

Dion and Janine laughed and leaned forward, ready to catch out his sleight of hand. Nothing ever got the better of Dion so he was all set to take the piss and explain to Janine how it was done. He sat as close as he could to Miles, ready to pounce and denounce him as a fraud.

Miles rolled up his sleeves, opened his hands palm up, then turned them over to show there was nothing hidden. Then he turned his hands over again and two coins were sitting in his palms. Janine looked impressed. No wonder the boys were so fascinated.

"It's all to do with the speed," Dion said. "You didn't give us chance to watch properly. Do it again slowly."

So Miles repeated the action in slow motion – and the coins were there in his hand. Janine laughed, not so much at the trick but at Dion's puzzled look and failure to catch him out.

Miles leant forward and took a coin from behind Dion's ear.

"Try this one," Miles said, shuffled the cards and dealt them all face down. "Ask me to pick any card."

"Two of hearts," Dion said. "That's for me and Janine."

Miles instantly found the two of hearts and they both looked incredulous.

"You've marked the cards somehow," Dion said and he scrutinised the backs of all of them and found nothing. He was not used to this feeling of being beaten.

It didn't matter how many cards they asked Miles to find, he turned the right one over immediately every time.

"What else can you do?" Dion asked, keen to catch him out somewhere to save face.

Miles spread his hands on the table, showed them palm upwards, placed them palm down, clicked his fingers, then turned his hands palm upwards to reveal the words Janine written on one hand, Dion on the other. They freaked.

Dion asked Miles to do the trick again and got as close as he could. Miles blew on his palms and their names disappeared, then repeated the trick again. Dion actually grabbed his hands, felt them and scrutinised them for clues.

"I'll do just one more," Miles said. "You two, come up with a word and I'll tell you what it is."

The sound of the truck rumbled on while they conferred. "We need something that isn't obvious," Dion said. "Think of something really random."

They turned their backs on him and wrote the word down so he wouldn't hear, making sure he couldn't see.

"It's 'cactus'," Miles said before they even turned round. Dion actually leapt and paced around.

"OK, let's talk," Dion said, his intuition telling him this would be one of the most important conversations of his life.

"I can do pretty much most things – so long as it doesn't involve aeroplanes or elephants," Miles said, "Though there are some people who can. I'm going to tell you something and if you ever repeat this to anyone, I will deny it."

The bus had paused at a crossroads and the sound of the engine ticking over mingled with their beating hearts.

"It's no coincidence we three work together. Dion, I know that since you have been a teenager you have known your destiny and I believe you have even seen it.

"Janine, strange things have followed you your whole life – and they intensified once Dion was on the scene.

"I look for people like you because I am the same. But I need to make a living. I could go on stage as a magician but I found a better way of making money – I earn it off the backs of special people like you. They are often gifted in some way, particularly musicians."

Janine was too dumbstruck to say a word. The bus had started up again and the drone was somehow comforting.

"Where do you think the music and lyrics come from?" Miles continued. "Where do you think a book writer gets inspiration for a story from? How do think a four-year-old prodigy can play the piano? You've heard people say they are 'gifted'. Well they are – gift wrapped in fact. That's what we call it."

Gift wrapped. There was that phrase again.

"That's what your mum told me about you," Janine said to Dion. "She said she was handing you to me, gift wrapped. She knows."

Miles leant forward so he could whisper, "Magic is real.

"They are not illusions; they are real, just like at your concerts. Do you think a magician could really do half the stuff he does unless it was real? And the Magic Circle knows that too. They say they are protecting how the tricks are done by not revealing the secrets; that's why they never tell the public. The real illusionists, not the crappy ones on talent shows, know the truth – but they're not about say that for fear of ridicule or what would happen to them because of national security."

"But why would you tell us this?" Janine said.

"Sometimes I come across special people and I feel they have a right to know. And I don't want you to be afraid, whatever happens. You are good together; you were meant to meet and you are sharing something wonderful with the world at the moment."

Dion felt as if things were starting to make sense. He had been thinking along some of those lines anyway.

"I have always felt out of step with the world," he said, "particularly before I met Janine."

"You were – are," Miles told him. "I can repeat my tricks to you a thousand times but you will never catch me out – because they are real."

"If this is true, how much control do we have over our lives?" Janine said.

"Not much," Miles answered. "The magic will take you where it wants, when the time is right. That's why so many gifted people, like you, leave this world too soon."

"Why would you say that to us?" Janine said, feeling as if she had been dragged straight back to that pillow talk day, fear rising from deep inside, then anger.

"Why are you being so cruel? I know there is stuff going on that's strange, but you shouldn't be saying that to someone who has two beautiful kids – or to Dion."

"Whatever happens is not up to me," Miles said. "We have a set path and there are some things you can't change. My feeling is Dion is very special and may find his way – if he hasn't already worked it out."

"This conversation never took place," he said. "I will deny it if you ever mention it to me or anyone else in the future. I just don't want either of you to be afraid. I love you both."

Then it was as if he clicked on a switch and the conversation never happened.

"Well, I'm turning in," he added. "Busy day tomorrow."

Janine sat fuming. Dion sat in quiet speculation, finishing his drink.

"Don't even ask where that came from," Dion said. "He's nuts. Fucking stupid magic tricks. Let's go to bed."

Chapter Thirty

When Dion and Janine got up about eleven a.m. the next day, the tour bus had already arrived at its next location and Miles was nowhere to be seen. He had done what he set out to do, so had taken the next flight back to the UK.

Neither of them wanted to talk about the previous night – and each had their own reasons, but there was no time to dwell on things anyway with preparations to be made for that night's gig. Much as they still loved what they did they were looking forward to returning home and it would be a year before they would back on the road.

The plan was to take a year out to write new material, go into the recording studio to make the next album and to work on a new video to promote the USA tour.

The last night of the tour in Germany was one to savour. The band members always marvelled at how foreign fans were word-perfect when it came to joining in the songs – and the *Magic of Rock* epic sounded particularly awesome that night. Everyone who left the building talked about a tingling feeling which they felt as they sang the song.

Janine had come into her own, refusing to be outshone by Dion. And though he always got his way off stage, she had by now managed to equal him performance-wise. She had agreed to some raunchy photo shoots without informing Dion, which did not go down well. But the resultant publicity was bringing her plenty of male attention and she decided to play Dion at his own game, keeping him on his toes.

"They only want to wank over your pictures at night," he told her when he picked up the glossy magazine. "Is that what you want?"

The thought made her feel physically ill but she wasn't going to admit that.

"Well, I'm sure that's what some guys do over your pictures," she said. "Is that what you want?"

She smiled to herself as he hurled the magazine into the hotel bin – and missed his aim.

'I'm getting better at this', she thought.

Such mini victories were rare – and they were all the more sweet for that. She didn't have any more racy photos taken, she had made her point; but for several months afterwards Dion had to contend with comments from guys who had seen the pictures, which were always met with a surly response.

As the band took their bows on the final night of the tour the sparkles reappeared on stage, like diamonds dispersed in the air, which made quite a spectacle.

The final image which the audience got to see was a huge projection on giant screens: a photo of Dion and Janine together looking happy, caught in a special moment laughing together.

Overlaid over the photo was the image of a giant two of hearts playing card, which might have been sweet had it not felt so chilling – to Janine in particular. But as ever the phenomena were no longer discussed, it was just accepted by the band and the audience saw it as a kind of tribute to the couple.

Back home, after a couple of weeks' rest plans were made for the video shoot. This was the third shoot they had agreed to do and Janine was dreading it, as it could be anywhere in the country and past experience told her it was going to be a nightmare.

Dion simply could not grasp the concept of being directed. The last two shoots had ended up complete fiascos due to his complete inability to accept what he was told to do. The second shoot in London went three times over budget due to Dion stropping off back to the hotel, leaving cast and crew fuming at their wasted time. Three directors later the video was finally completed.

Dion always wanted the video to reflect the song in some way but had a pathological hatred of anything he saw as 'contrived'. Attempts to get him to pose with his hair blowing in fake wind failed miserably. Janine cringed as the director tried to persuade him to lie on a bed surrounded by semi naked women. It wasn't the naked women he objected to, but the fact that it had nothing to do with the song.

Among the failures were: trying to get him to sit astride a motorbike dressed in leather; trying to dress him in a suit; suggesting he wore a hat; getting him to run down a street in the rain; posing with a rifle; lying on a sunbed looking wasted with drug paraphernalia around him. In fact it was easier to say what he wouldn't do, rather than what he would do.

Janine looked on with her head in her hands as directors tried to reason with Dion when he had said a flat 'No'. It usually ended with something like, 'Which part of 'no' did you not understand'? or 'I'm going for a fag. Let me know when you've got your act together'.

He still only ever smoked when under stress, so always went armed with several packets of fags for every video shoot, knowing he would be spending most of his time outside fuming, literally.

Janine often tried to gently suggest to directors that it would save time and money if they just agreed with him – but directors had their own egos and there were so many clashes.

With the video shoot finally over, and way over budget again, everyone in the band returned home for a break, thankful that they would not have to see him again until the recording session which was due in a few weeks.

Dion and Janine settled into some kind of normality in the village where they lived. She could not help but be amused at the sight of him walking Rolo down the country lanes as if he was a perfectly normal local resident. Janine got a real kick out of seeing middle class local ladies acknowledge their newly adopted, long-haired, totally out of place neighbour with, 'Morning, Mr Freeman'. She found that hysterical.

By and large the villagers left them alone and they were even able to enjoy a drink with mates at the local Park Gate Inn, sitting by the warm, friendly open fire.

After enjoying a well-earned break from Dion the band came together for rehearsal sessions at his home studio.

Dion announced that the twins should now take a more 'up front' role. He argued that vocally they were good enough, that they looked great, knew the songs inside out and the band had never given them enough prominence.

It was agreed they would start by taking over front vocals for a couple of the songs at each performance, with a view to increasing this later, which would also give Dion and Janine a break.

What the twins hadn't expected was that he ordered extra rehearsal sessions for them at his studio, where he grilled them mercilessly and made them go over and over the songs until he was satisfied they were performing with enough attitude and aggression.

The latest album was recorded at a state of the art London studio. They were happy with the new edgy material and were itching to get back on the road again. The video to accompany the album featured the band performing on a stage, with short clips of new footage which were appropriate to the song. Enough said.

Miles sent details of the US tour with dates and schedule. It was two-year run, with time to come home three times a year. It would be their most punishing yet but Dion was well up for it, saying he admired the Yanks for their 'Anything possible, just do it' attitude. Everyone seemed to have a renewed energy and was looking forward to getting back on the road.

All the publicity material nowadays referred to 'Dion'. Unlike the rest of the band, his surname was never used, as if everyone knew who he was anyway.

The night before setting off for the US Dion was in a good mood. He had just arranged several VIP passes and free travel for his mates for some of the venues and was hyper with energy.

But to Janine it was a sobering thought that towards the end of the USA tour he would be approaching his 39th birthday.

With the kids in their rooms doing their own stuff and everything ready for the following day's departure, Dion announced at ten p.m., "Let's have an early night." But the look in his eyes told Janine he had no intention of sleeping. Both happy to sink into the luxury of their own bed, they spent a couple of hours enjoying each other. Some of their happiest times were spent lying next to each other, side by side, resting their heads on soft, white pillows, exhausted after sex and talking long into the night. It was at these times they whispered words of love, two soul mates in the semi darkness.

"I love watching you come when I'm on top," Janine told him in a tone that was a mix of love and mischief. She was moving the hair out of his eyes yet again as she spoke. "I love watching that face, with your eyes closed and the way you look when you are lost in pleasure."

He groaned and pulled her close, feeling turned on again by her words.

"The only time I ever see anything which comes close is when you are mid-way through a guitar lead-break on stage, completely in the zone," she added. "And I love the way you hold my hands tight in those last moments, interlinking your fingers in mine, until you relax and look so peaceful."

"I do the same with you," he said, his hands wandering down her body. "I love listening to you and I always watch your face; I find it so erotic."

And they laughed at finding out something new about each other after all these years. After all, how could they have known they watched each other? They would each have had their eyes closed at the time.

Chapter Thirty-One

The USA more than lived up to Dion's expectations. He loved the attitude, the vast countryside and the colossal stadiums.

But the, 'Have a nice day' and what he called 'crap TV' drove him crazy.

He also started as he meant to go on, by saying exactly what he wanted on national TV. The backlash caught him somewhat by surprise as he found their puritanical attitude confusing. On the one hand they were really up for anything; on the other it was, 'You can't say this', or, 'You can't say that', which was never going to work for Dion.

Janine's boys, even though they were in their late teens, still toured with the band, loving the lifestyle and fiercely proud of their mum. Dion took them on as roadies, and although he was filthy rich by now, paid them the same as all the others. He knew that in some time in the future they would inherit a fortune; for now he wanted them to be as grounded as possible.

Throughout the tour all the band members were keen to give up-and-coming talent a shot at performing on the big stage. Many bands jumped at the chance and benefitted from such a high profile opportunity. Dion gave the sound crew instructions that support bands should have equal sound quality to Son of Gabriel so they could show their potential. Sometimes he would watch the bands during the sound check, which always made the front man (or woman) hyperventilate with nerves. Sometimes he listened from backstage or watched from the wings. The lights man gave the support band all the treatment, since no phenomena ever occurred when they were on stage.

Son on Gabriel was well into the tour by the time they set up in Chicago. An American band called Jo-Dan Rox would have the support slot for one of the nights. Dion liked the name, thought it was cool, so decided to check them out. He sat with the sound guy out front, thinking a bit of intimidation might actually do them good.

Everything was set up ready to go and the support band had about twenty minutes for a run-through. Dion watched, intrigued, as the front man, only in his twenties, romped through the first number of a blistering set, seemingly unfazed by his high profile audience. He was of average height, super fit with black, glossy, shoulder length hair which seemed to bounce with a life of its own as he leapt around the stage. His voice range was phenomenal and his lead guitar work was streets ahead of anything Dion could achieve.

"This guy's good," he said to his sound man.

What also stood out was his arrogant on-stage presence and Dion liked him all the more for that. This guy had a confidence beyond his years and with the expertise of Dion's sound crew, his vocals sounded awesome.

Dion was puzzled when the front man indicated for the band to stop playing mid-way through their next song.

"Hey, how about we have some more volume in the monitors?" he shouted at the sound guy. "And I need some more cut on my lead."

"Sounds fine to me," the technician fed back to him on the mic.

"Well it's not how I'd like it," came the response. "Do you think you could be adaptable?"

The sound guy looked sideways at Dion. "Fuck, who does that remind you of?" he said. He and Dion had experienced many a clash at the start of their first tour before they could agree on the sound quality.

"OK, I'll make some adjustments," the sound guy fed back to him in an irritated voice.

"I should fuckin' hope so," came back the response, resulting in the sound guy showing a clenched fist to Dion.

The band finished the set – and the kid had been right. The sound was much improved.

The singer leapt off the stage after their sound check and lit up a fag - underneath the huge 'no smoking' sign by an exit door.

Dion went over to him, intrigued to get to know him, expecting to find the guy was actually nicer than his on-stage persona.

"Hey, you're good," he said. And this was the first time he had paid such a compliment. "That your real name, Jo-Dan, or is it made up?"

"No more made up than Dee-on," he said, emphasising the name so that it sounded elongated and ridiculous.

"That is my real name – and it's pronounced Dion," he replied. He actually liked that he had a slightly unusual name and hated the way the American had pronounced it.

"What's your plan with the band? Where do you see yourself going?" Dion asked.

"World domination," Jo-Dan answered, looking directly at Dion and blowing smoke into his face.

The conversation was overheard by one of the roadies, who scuttled off out of the way, anticipating one almighty punch was about to be forthcoming.

Dion stood opposite Jo-Dan, unflinching as the smoke got into his throat, but he was trying not to show he had been rattled. In truth, had it been physically possible you would have seen smoke coming out of his ears, he was so mad.

"Your sound man's shit," the American drawled.

"You know, some bands are actually grateful they've got this support slot," Dion said quietly, impressed by his own composure under the circumstances.

"Whatever," came the response with a shrug. "I'm gonna make it anyway."

And he took a long drag on the fag and blew it directly into Dion's face.

"Do you smoke?" Jo-Dan asked.

"No," Dion replied grabbing him by his T shirt and shoving him against the wall. "It affects my voice." He was trying to give some advice, from one singer to another, but was now actually shaking with rage.

Jo-Dan fixed his dark brown eyes on Dion without blinking.

"I was named after a kick-ass move in martial arts," he said. "And I'm gonna kick your ass off stage tonight."

Dion tightened the grip on his T shirt as he stood face to face with him.

"Pity you're such a wanker," he said and walked away.

"Better watch your ass, Dee-on," Jo-Dan shouted after him. "I'm coming up behind you."

It took Dion an hour and several cigarettes to calm down before he resolved to bide his time. He was even madder that he had let the guy get to him and that he had been driven back to smoking, albeit temporarily.

The crowd that night was really up for it. Jo-Dan Rox had never performed in front of such a huge audience. The lights went down, the support band's pounding intro tape came on and the singer came out all guns blazing, full of energy and sounding awesome.

Dion was standing in the wings, wearing a head set with a microphone and as he watched this young band, he suddenly felt thirty-eight years old.

Jo-Dan caught sight of him and punched the air in triumph, knowing he had the crowd in the palm of his hands. Dion spoke into the mic – and the sound went completely dead. Jo-Dan's last few words sounded feeble in the vast auditorium and he looked mortified.

Dion punched the air in full view of him.

The sound came back on – and just as the singer was getting into his stride again it cut out completely. The audience looked unsettled and started to boo.

Dion was amusing himself talking into the mic to the sound guy.

The sound came back on and Jo-Dan went into a complete rant about how support bands had to put up with this shit – and he was allowed to go on and on – hanging himself when the audience got fed up and started to chuck beer cans at him.

Dion signalled to the support band's musicians to start playing again, which they did, struggling on without any vocals.

The sight of Jo-Dan having a massive tantrum on the stage like a three-year-old almost made Dion piss himself, he was laughing so hard. And when the singer hurled his mic on the floor of the stage and stamped on his guitar Dion mimed the universal 'wanker' sign at him from the wings.

Jo-Dan was raging. He stormed off the stage and launched for Dion, who by now was taking a long drag of a cigarette under a huge 'no smoking' sign. Two burly security guys held the singer tight as Dion blew the smoke full into his face before he was hauled away, kicking, punching and screaming obscenities. The front rows of the audience just managed to hear something about C U Next Tuesday and a torrent of abuse about Dion's mother before he was slung out of the side doors into the rain.

Jo-Dan's band carried on with their set apologetically, with full sound restored, but without their front man. There was no encore.

Dion went off to the dressing room to get ready for the concert, laughing to himself on the way. Tommy was there, drumming on the tables as he often did while waiting to go on stage.

"Hey," Dion said as he joined him then sat quietly, watching him tap out a beat.

Tommy stopped after a while and looked up. "You're quiet, you OK?"

"You know, mate, if anything ever happens to me, you must keep the band going," Dion replied.

Taken aback by this statement out of the blue, Tommy looked puzzled.

"What do mean, if anything happens to you? What you on about?"

"Well, if I fell off stage and broke my neck or something."

"Are you tired? What's got into you? You're acting weird."

"I'm just saying, you never know," Dion said and went quiet again, listening to the faint background music playing for the interval.

"And if I do ever stop performing, for whatever reason, I've found the perfect guy to front this band. Promise me you'll take him on. Here's his contact details," he said, handing Tommy a card. "He's perfect, trust me."

Tommy looked at the name on the card: Jo-Dan Rox.

"What, that asshole who was on earlier? I've heard about his sound check."

"Promise me," Dion insisted.

"I'll promise if it makes you happy," Tommy said, giving him a sideways look that said, 'You sure you're OK'?"

"And, Tommy?"

"Yea, what?" he said.

"You know I love you, man."

"I love you too, mate," Tommy said. "Think you need a rest. It's a good job we've got a break coming up soon."

Dion sat staring into a mirror for a few awkward minutes then shook himself out of his melancholy mood, psyching himself up for the concert.

"And don't repeat this conversation to anyone in the band yet – please," he added as he went off to find Janine.

Tommy nodded and went back to his drumming on the table.

Chapter Thirty-Two

Tommy had been right; it really was time for a break – for everyone.

By the end of that leg of the USA tour everyone was shattered. Each time they packed up for home it was a weary experience, but one they looked forward to.

But as the tour ground on, with all the travelling involved, even the to-ing and fro-ing back to Britain was starting to take its toll.

Each time they returned to the States it was as if they had an on/off switch. They could still turn it on for the performances, but the energy drained away by the end of each leg of the tour.

The 'special effects' continued to cause a stir. Silver 'sparkles' appeared randomly around the auditorium, fizzing like sparklers at a bonfire party just for a second, then disappearing, only to reappear somewhere else. Fans would try to catch them, but they were always just out of reach.

Dion's mic stand would light up and become luminescent. The first time it happened he let go of the mic sharply, convinced he was about to be electrocuted, but gradually he got used to the ever changing colours.

Now misty holograms were appearing at the back of the stage, bearing a resemblance to icons such as Elvis, James Dean and Marc Bolan. The audience was entranced by the 'technology' which could bring heroes back but Janine found it freaky, often feeling as if she was performing with ghosts.

The band and its publicity machine continued relentlessly, so on the last but one flight home everyone was elated – because they could see the end in sight.

"We go home, have a great time, then come back and smash it," Dion told the band. "We'll go out on a high on the last leg of the tour."

For now they had a precious month back home and all Dion could think of was getting back to Rolo.

When they returned to Cannock Wood you would have sworn that Rolo performed a dance of delight; he was so pleased to see Dion and they immediately went for a tear around the garden together, playing ball.

Janine smiled as she watched them; she so loved to see Dion happy.

The month-long break was picture postcard perfect. When the boys were not visiting their dad, they sat in the studio with Dion learning Son of Gabriel songs. Although they had no intention of performing, it was a fun time for the three of them and a way of Dion being able to keep his hand in while he was off the road.

There were also visits to the Park Gate Inn, usually on a weekday when the pub was mostly full of locals. They had got to know many of the locals by now and enjoyed spending time with them and Dion was happy that Rolo was allowed in too. One of the regulars jokingly complained that Dion and Janine had performed in Europe and the USA, but the pub regulars had only ever seen them on TV or in videos, never 'live'.

"Give 'em a break," the barman had said. "They're back home to rest, let them chill out."

But walking back home, with one arm holding Rolo on a lead and the other arm round Janine Dion said, "You know, they're right. We should do an acoustic set for them."

So the next time they visited the pub Dion told the regulars that he and Janine would perform just for them the following Tuesday night. Janine set out first that night, Dion saying he would catch up with her later as he had some phone calls to make.

When she arrived, the pub was packed. Word had got round. Many of the customers had invited friends or family to what was supposed to have been a small scale event. Janine felt a little nervous, preferring to perform in front of thousands of strangers than to a small audience of people she knew.

She had a couple of drinks to calm her nerves and chatted to staff and customers as she waited for Dion to arrive.

One of the customers, who was a near neighbour, had brought a friend with her, a beautiful girl with straight long, blond hair.

"This is Helga, my niece, her neighbour told her. "She is a real fan and plays bass guitar so she's really looking forward to hearing you both."

"Hi, Helga," Janine said looking at the girl's twenty-year-old flawless skin.

"I'm so pleased to meet you," Helga said, a bit breathlessly. "I'm such a fan."

Janine sometimes forgot when she was at home the effect which she and Dion could have on people.

"And I can't wait to see Dion, he looks amazing. I was watching your latest video last night and thought how stunning he looks – for a guy who's nearly forty."

Helga went babbling on, but all Janine could hear were those last words.

"Please don't say that to him, about looking good for his age, when he arrives," she told her, trying to sound jokey. "He's actually very vain."

"But it's a compliment," Helga said. "You look amazing too. How do you do it?"

"Thank you, it's all down to sex, booze and rock and roll," she joked. "But trust me," Janine said firmly, "he would not take your comments as a compliment."

When Dion walked through the door he still managed to take Janine's breath away. He was wearing tight black trousers, tucked into his favourite ankle high, black buckled boots with a simple black and red T shirt which had a few sparkly bits on it. His hair was longer than any female's in the pub; and to add to the rock star image he was carrying one of his many guitars.

Looking a bit surprised by the crowd, he searched the room for Janine and smiled when he caught her eye.

Helga looked totally dumbstruck and fortunately was unable to say anything intelligible when introduced to Dion.

It turned out to be one of those special magical nights that people talk about for years. Dion was in fine form and more than happy to play and sing their songs together, acoustic style. It reminded Janine of the intimate time they sat on the bed together in the George Hotel, harmonising, just the two of them, a world away.

It was about midnight by the time they returned home that night, happy and tired – but never too tired to make love until the early hours. Usually after such sessions they would lie in until about ten a.m. so Janine was surprised to be awaken in what seemed like the middle of the night.

"Jan, are you awake?" Dion said curled around her back.

She looked at the bedside clock which told her it was four a.m.

"Oh, God," she thought. She knew what, 'Are you awake?' usually meant and she felt exhausted, but not once in her life had she turned him away.

"Uh-huh," she said sleepily, slowly turning round to face him.

"I just need a hug," he said and burst into tears.

Janine was suddenly wide awake. She had only ever seen him cry twice in all the years they had been together: once in the hospital and once on stage at the Garrick Theatre, both of them completely understandable.

"What on earth is the matter?" she asked pulling him to her, but fearing he was about to break the news of an affair or something terrible.

"Nothing's the matter. Everything is perfect," he said and he cried himself to sleep as she held him.

Chapter Thirty-Three

Janine hardly slept at all that night. She got up, made coffee, went back to bed and sat up reading, waiting for Dion to wake.

When he eventually stirred sleepily she snuggled down next to him for 'pillow talk'.

"Morning," she said stroking his hair.

"Hi, mistress," he said sleepily, running his fingers along her arm.

He pulled her towards him and she lay quietly on his chest for a while listening to him breathing.

Then, unable to bear it any longer she propped herself up on her elbow, looked him in the eye and asked gently, "What was all that about last night?" searching his face for a reaction.

"I don't want to go back on the road," he said almost guiltily. "I've had enough. I've achieved everything I set out to do and I just want to be with you."

"But we have to go back, we have a contract to fulfil and so many people's jobs depend on us," she said. "And it's the last lap – then you can make some changes if you want."

He seemed to think about this for a minute.

"Can we go away somewhere, just by ourselves, after the tour, Jan?"

"I would love that," she said, impressed that he had asked and not demanded – and he looked immediately happier.

"Can I have a coffee?" he asked.

"Yes, since you asked so nicely," Janine said. "You're learning. Usually it's, 'We are going somewhere or get me a coffee'."

So they returned to the USA, but not before Janine saw him cry once more – as he said goodbye to Rolo.

"God, he loves that dog more than me," she said to her boys. "I'm sure he wouldn't cry that much if he was saying goodbye to me."

The last leg of the tour took the band to Los Angeles where everyone enjoyed days off, exploring iconic sights.

The hotel suite in LA was particularly beautiful, one of the best Dion and Janine had ever stayed in and the band members were impressed by the local attractions and restaurants.

"What do you want to do for your birthday?" Janine asked as they stretched out by the hotel pool - expecting him to reply, 'Nothing, I hate birthdays, what's there to celebrate about being thirty-nine'?

But she was taken totally by surprise when he said enthusiastically, "I've decided I will celebrate. Tommy says there's this great restaurant downtown. It'd be good to let our hair down and we could take all the band and crew. I'll make sure everyone gets there first and they can have drinks on me until I make my grand entrance. After all, it's my day."

Janine laughed at his inflated ego.

'Blimey', she thought to herself. 'Perhaps I'll even be allowed to buy a present this time'. Normally he would rant along the lines of, 'What do I need a present for? I've got everything I could possibly need'. (True.)

"So," she said carefully, "Is there anything you would like as a present?"

"Yes," came the reply. "I'd like a silver ring with two diamonds set in it. I thought it would look good with my bracelet now I'm all tanned."

"Well, that was very specific," she said.

"And I'll open it at the meal in the afternoon, let everyone admire it. Make sure it's expensive."

His precise instructions were not that unusual. Dion had a hatred of shopping. If he really had to go he would hurl stuff in the trolley without looking at the price, just keen to get out of the place. He used to shop in that way even before he was famous, when he did not have a lot of money. And at work at the record shop he would wait for someone to go for lunch so they would fetch his, too.

Now as a rich rock star, Dion would give his orders in great detail about what he wanted. He could never be bothered to go himself, but he would send the twins or anyone else who would listen to buy his clothes or whatever. But they would have to stand and listen to a string of instructions along the lines of, 'And it's got to have this or that', or, 'It better not have such and such', or 'And I don't want one of those that are—'.

If the reverse happened and they tried to describe anything they had seen in the shops in great detail back to him he would reply with, "I don't care. Stop talking, I'm bored now," and walk off.

A week later, on his thirty-nineth birthday Dion got up late as usual, grudgingly accepted 'happy birthday' greetings with his coffee but opened no cards, saying he'd open them later with his present. Luckily Janine had managed to get him to sit still long enough to establish his ring size.

But he was looking forward to the meal. He said, "It's a posh restaurant apparently, so I suppose I'd better scrub up and wear something decent," – meaning a flowing shirt and jeans rather than a T shirt and jeans.

"What shall I wear?" Janine asked, knowing it was hopeless question as he never took any interest, saying she always looked great anyway.

"Wear that long silver dress you bought. I like that," he said, catching her by surprise. It was a kind of figure hugging, silky, slinky dress that she had bought the previous week and only worn once.

At about one p.m. they were ready, Dion looking stunning in a white flowing shirt which had a small motif of little silver stars on it. So, with her gift in her handbag they took a cab to the restaurant.

Janine wondered why the cab had pulled up in front of a tiny white chapel and why everyone was standing outside.

The driver held the door open for her and she stepped out to cheers. Someone thrust a bouquet of silver flowers into her hand while Dion turned to her and said, "Give the ring to my best man. We are getting married."

"What?" (There was that incredulous 'what' again).

Tommy took the ring and the next half an hour went by like some fantasy.

Janine repeated some words which disappeared in a haze and stood in the chapel while Dion made a prepared speech about how much he adored her, called her his soul mate, apologised for being a total nightmare to live with and said he wanted to spend the rest of his life with her.

He told her she was beautiful and said even their initials, D and J, DJ, sounded like they made music together which resulted in a collective 'aahhhh' from the guests and made Janine cry.

Dion placed a beautiful, delicate silver ring on her finger which was inlaid with two diamonds, then it was his turn to cry as she placed his birthday/wedding ring, designed as instructed, on the third finger of his left hand.

"I now pronounce you man and wife. You may kiss the bride."

Dion went for it enthusiastically, much to the amusement of everyone and they laughed as he announced the kiss had included 'tongues'.

"You can keep your surname if you want," he told Janine as he led her off to sign the register. "That's your stage name. That's who you are."

Still quite unable to take in what had just happened Janine then found herself getting into a beautiful white car and being whisked away to the 'posh restaurant'.

Dion leant over to her in the car and said, "I love you, my wife; I'll have to stop calling you my mistress now. This is the only gift I wanted for my birthday."

'Wife, that sounds extraordinary', Mrs Janine Lee thought.

She spent the afternoon in a haze of happy chatter. It seemed no-one in the band and crew, except for Tommy, knew about the wedding, in a bid to avoid publicity. Guests who had been told and were sworn to secrecy included Dion's parents, his ex boss, his mates from home, Janine's boys, brother and sister and Miles. They had all been instructed not to buy wedding gifts; and everyone had been told not to buy birthday gifts.

Everyone had met up at the restaurant which was booked as a private function for the day, then discreet-looking coaches had arrived to take them to and from the church.

Dion wanted the whole occasion to be as informal as possible, so the only other speech was a short one by him. He thanked all the guests for being there, said he loved everyone in that room and that he would remember the day forever.

Janine slowly let the experience of her wedding day sink in during their four-day honeymoon and absolute peace at a Malibu hotel, where Dion told her his recent emotional scenes had all been down to planning the wedding.

It seemed as if he had thought of everything. Even Rolo was being taken care of, enjoying life by the fire at the Park Gate Inn.

"What will you dream up for your 40th birthday?" Janine asked him tentatively as they lay in bed on the last morning of their honeymoon.

"I'll think of something," he replied.

She felt an overwhelming sense of relief as he hugged her close.

"And is there a particular reason you wanted us to have two diamonds on our rings?"

"Because that's what Mum chose for my bracelet," he said. "When she bought it for my 30th birthday she told me the diamonds reminded her of stars. She said she would think of me every night when she was in Spain looking up at the sky."

Janine felt a tug of pity for his mum but Dion looked accepting of the situation.

"I also wanted that design on the rings because that's what we are: two stars," he added with a complete lack of modesty.

Dion's mum and dad, his ex boss, the boys and Miles would be staying for a few weeks' holiday to catch the band's final USA performance.

And they would watch two stars, man and wife, give the performance of their lives.

Chapter Thirty-Four

Dion took a deep breath as he lay on the hotel bed and dialled the number.

It was two p.m. so he figured the little punk would be just about up by now.

The phone answered with a sleepy, "Yea?" as if the guy wasn't sure who was calling him.

"Hi. Jo-Dan? It's Dion."

"Of course it is," Jo-Dan said sarcastically – and put the phone down.

Dion was fuming already and he had hardly spoken a few words to him.

He rang back and tried again and Jo-Dan answered with an irritated, "What?"

"It really is Dion, you prick – or Dee-on as you like to call me."

Jo-Dan was suddenly wide awake, thinking, 'Shit, this is one of the world's most iconic singers ringing me', but he wasn't about to admit that.

"Yea, what-d-ya want?"

Dion took another deep breath and considered lighting a cigarette.

"I want to ask you a question."

"Go on."

"Do you take drugs?"

"What's it to do with you? Why would you ring me to blurt that out?"

"Do you?"

"No. I get high on music," Jo-Dan replied, so emphatically that Dion believed him.

"How well do you know my songs?"

'Another strange question', Jo-Dan thought.

"I know every breath, every word and every note," he said, cursing himself for sounding sycophantic, but man, he loved Dion's music.

"I'm thinking of having a guest spot on our last night in LA. Would you like to take over vocals on one of our songs during the concert?"

"What, so you can have your sound guy cut the mic and humiliate me again?" he replied, still angry.

"What if I promise that won't happen?"

"Yea, and I'm expected to believe you?"

"Look, you little bastard, I'm trying to offer you another chance here. What song do you like best?"

"*Thank You For the Ride*," he answered, now starting to believe this offer might actually be real. His band had gone nowhere fast since the last fiasco with Dion.

"No can do," Dion said. "We're using that for the encore. What else?"

"*Marathon Man*," he said.

"OK. *Marathon Man* it is. D'you wanna come for a rehearsal next Friday afternoon to run through it with the band before the concert?"

"No. I don't need to rehearse," Jo-Dan said. "I'll just do it on the night."

"Fine," Dion answered, seriously peed off by his cockiness. "See you just before the performance. There'll be a pass for you on the door."

Then he put the phone down and went on a desperate search for a packet of fags.

When Janine caught up with him later in the day he was chain smoking like someone possessed.

"Back on them?" she said.

"Spoke to Jo-Dan on the phone," he answered, raising his eyes to the heavens.

"Oh. Enough said," Janine answered.

Dion had told the band about Jo-Dan's appearance and they looked surprised, but thought, 'Well it's only one song', so resolved to put up with him.

And when Dion continued chain smoking daily in the run up to the final performance Janine put it down to him working on a new on-stage backdrop which he was keeping under wraps – and his irritation at having to deal with Jo-Dan.

"I've got an idea for a new stage backdrop," Dion had told Janine a few days before the gig. "I'm going to use it in the finale; it'll be a surprise. I think you'd like it." And he refused to say any more.

The night before the gig, still chain smoking, Dion announced that he would like an early night. Janine knew what 'early night' meant and as he had also drunk considerably from about six p.m. she knew she was in for it.

They were in bed for about nine p.m. and by midnight she was exhausted – and so was her husband. Dion was never one to have any inhibitions, but fuelled by alcohol, he was more passionate than ever. So when the inevitable question "Jan, are you awake?" came at four a.m. she thought she was about to refuse him for the first time ever. But he whispered how much he loved her over and over, called her his beautiful wife.

He knew her body so well that he was able to arouse her all over again. Eventually, as she was about to fall into grateful sleep, he whispered to her, "Jan. I've put the house in the kids' names and I've transferred millions into their accounts."

Janine was aware that he had spoken these words but in her exhausted state she just wanted to sleep. Anyway, even if he had given millions away, he would still have millions, so she simply replied, "I'll talk to you tomorrow," and drifted off.

The following morning she dragged herself out of bed feeling like death. Dion was smoking on the balcony, looking lost in thought, so she poured a coffee and joined him.

"Mornin'," she said, sitting in the sunlight next to him and shading her eyes.

"Hey," he said gently touching her messy hair. "I thought I'd let you sleep."

She thought he looked a bit worse for wear after the copious amounts of alcohol from the night before.

"Yea, thanks for that," she said, attempting sarcasm. "What was that you said in the early hours about the house and millions of pounds? Did I dream that or did you really say it? You see, the thing with you is, you say outrageous things that most people would not believe, but I know you. When you say something you do it. Tell me I was dreaming."

He just stared straight ahead at the view of LA stretching for miles.

"Of course I've done it," he said without looking at her. "It's for the boys' eighteenth and twenty-first birthdays. Why wouldn't I give them something special?"

"But where are we supposed to live?"

"We'll find another place – and I'm sure they'll let us stay anyway. We'll visit the boys and Rolo often.

"Haven't told them yet, but they'll find the details in the post when they get back home. Don't tell them; let it be a surprise."

End of conversation.

'Oh, God', Janine sighed to herself. 'Now I'll have all that disruption moving house'.

But she consoled herself that Dion had promised they would go away together, straight after tonight's gig. She could worry about it after their holiday. She was still too tired to deal with it now.

By late afternoon everyone was just finishing the sound check when Jo-Dan swaggered in to watch.

"God, those three are hot," he said to Dion before even saying hello. And he was holding his crotch as if to say, 'I could have any of them'.

It took every ounce of control for Dion not to punch him.

"Do you deliberately try to annoy me or are you just so up your own ass that you don't realise?" Dion said. "That's my wife you are talking about – and I can tell you for sure you are not their type. If you disrespect any of those girls tonight I will not only have your mic cut, I will personally cut off your balls, do you understand?"

"Cool it, man. You sound like my dad. I was just sayin'—"

"Well, don't," Dion said and stormed off for a fag.

As he sat smoking, trying to calm down, his mind wandered. It crossed his mind that the names Dion and Jan contained almost all the same letters as Jo-Dan. Then he started to think about Janine and how she had spent time listening to her boys' favourite music with them yesterday and how happy she looked with them. His heart lurched.

It was customary for the band to get together just before the concert on last nights, when they would form a circle for a 'group hug'. Dion would usually give his thanks to them for all their hard work and energise them with some well chosen words. On this night his words were heartfelt and touching. He hugged each one individually, particularly Tommy, who eventually protested with, "Get off me, man. You're not my type."

He told them all to have a long holiday before they would return to the stage.

They could hear the capacity crowd and even backstage the atmosphere was electric. Jo-Dan was in the wings, looking at the audience, completely awestruck. He had yet to switch on his pretend bravado.

Janine's boys would be enjoying the concert from the wings tonight with Dion's parents; Miles and other guests were out front.

This was it; one last push.

And it was wild; the band and the audience were as one. The band had performed the songs so often now that they came naturally and they instinctively knew what each other was doing. The contrasts between up tempo and ballads worked their magic; the crowd was noisy, adoring and word-perfect; and the phenomena added to the spectacle of the night.

About half way through the concert Dion took the luminescent mic, shushed the audience with one gesture of his hand and announced, "OK. Now we have a special guest for the next number. You are gonna hear a lot more about this guy in the future. Please welcome – Jo-Dan Rox."

There was not a hint of any displeasure from Dion; in fact he screamed out Jo-Dan's name to give him a dramatic introduction.

Jo-Dan launched himself onto the stage with not a hint of nerves. He sang and played guitar with absolute confidence, reached all the high notes with ease and had even changed some parts which he felt needing improving.

He played to the audience, giving eye contact to the front rows, raced from one side of the stage to the other throughout the performance, pulled off some impressive rock posing and still found time to sidle up to the three girls suggestively, making them laugh and respond.

Dion kept a watchful eye at that point to make sure he didn't cross the line, especially with Janine.

The applause he received was rapturous.

Miles was captivated by the pink and blue aura which surrounded Jo-Dan throughout his performance. No-one else saw it, but he did – and he was already counting the pound signs.

"Told you I'd kick your ass off stage," Jo-Dan said to Dion as they crossed paths on the stage.

Dion decided to let him have his moment.

"You did that," he shouted to him over the continuing roar of the crowd.

"Hey, Dion!" Jo-Dan shouted back as he started to exit (actually pronouncing his name correctly, albeit in an American accent).

243

Dion prepared himself for some crass comment to arrive.

"Thanks," Jo-Dan said.

The rest of the set went up a notch as the band launched into their most popular songs.

The 'special effect' sparkles were madder than usual, Dion thought. The fast paced swirling reminded him of the beautiful sight of birds swooping and diving in synchronisation – all individual, but as one.

Son of Gabriel took their triumphant final bow, with Jo-Dan, after their encore, but returned for a second encore with *Thank You For the Ride*.

Right at the end of the song the band usually jammed an elongated section before Tommy crashed in on the drums which was the signal to end.

As the session started the roar of the crowd was deafening.

The sparkles were in tighter formation. Dion watched as they became closer and denser, leaving the audience and circling around the stage.

He leant his guitar up against an amp and quickly grabbed Janine from behind as she prepared to take a bow – and he was shaking. Janine watched as the sparkly effect began to concentrate around them and her instinct was to run away.

But Dion held her close, his arms wrapped around her, his fingers linked tightly across her waist.

'What's he doing'? she thought, irritated with him for fooling about with her so publicly.

The jamming session continued and the sparkly lights, which were like crystals reflecting the sun, were now only around Dion and Janine.

Her boys were laughing. They had really enjoyed the concert and now they were amused by Dion doing his usual playful hug. They knew how much this always irritated their mum and they could just make her out inside the lights, struggling desperately to free herself from him and trying to stamp on his feet. They imagined him saying to her, 'Say you love me three times and I'll let you go'.

They did not realise she was fighting Dion as if her life depended on it - because it did. Janine was trying to get away because she really was frightened. She had realised that as the sparkly lights became more and more dense, there was no gap to get out, but Dion was determined to stop her from escaping.

Janine could hear the muffled sound of the band and the crowd, but inside the sphere it was quiet and time hung in the air.

What seemed like a minute to those watching from outside was equivalent to about five minutes inside the sphere.

And as it closed them in, Dion slowly let go of her waist, turned her to face him and looked deeply into her eyes.

"It's time," he said gently. "We have to go."

A peaceful look had come over his face, so peaceful that it reminded her of the 'special face' they had talked about. He was breathing slowly and deeply, his eyes were closing and he looked as if he was in ecstasy. She could hear every shuddering breath clearly, while the noise continued 'outside'.

"Can you feel it?" Dion said, now overcome with waves of something beautiful. He fixed his ice blue eyes onto her and whispered, "I have to go now. Come with me. We are magic together."

Janine remembered how he had talked about 'a place' and she now felt sick with fear.

He pulled her close, interlinked his fingers with hers and searched her eyes for a response. She could feel him gradually being pulled away from her. Then she felt it too – an intense pull to 'somewhere else'.

"I can't get out," she said in a panic.

"As soon as we go, this – whatever this is – will collapse and disappear. Trust me," he said,

And he closed his eyes, totally lost in his experience, but trying to hold her hands tight.

The band was still playing the last bars of the song outside. From inside, in their alternative time zone, it felt as if the music was going on forever.

As Dion's fingers started to slip away from hers it reminded her of the night outside the Arts Centre, when he lost his grip on her hand and left her for three and a half months.

"Dion. You don't have to go," she screamed, trying to startle him back to her. "You are making this happen because you want it to, but it doesn't have to be this way. Stay with me and the boys and we'll be happy."

Then she felt a wave of euphoria sweep over her, washing over her again and again, pulling at her. And she understood; she saw the place; not a place she could describe in words, but somewhere creative and beautiful.

Dion could see the fear in her eyes and it hurt him so much he found it difficult to watch. But he tightened his grip on her hands again. "Don't be afraid," he said. "Miles said we shouldn't be afraid. I want to go, but please don't let me go on my own." And his voice sounded increasingly desperate as he knew time was running out.

The guitars thrashed away outside.

They could both feel such a wave of love and euphoria for each other but Janine was also being tugged in another direction – to her boys.

"I can't choose between you and my boys!" she cried, desperate now. "Please don't leave me. I love you so much. Please don't do this."

The waves were now washing over him every few seconds and they were taking his breath away. Dion tried desperately to persuade her to just let go.

Then he turned her round, telling her to look at her boys. He pressed himself tightly against her back and put his arm around her waist; he buried his head in her hair and could feel the essence of her. She could feel his breathing was erratic now.

"Look at your boys, look at your boys, look at your boys," he kept repeating in a desperate attempt to distract her. "Look how happy they are. Look how beautiful they are. They will be fine. I'm sorry. I'm sorry. I'm so sorry."

Janine watched her boys, still laughing at what they thought was Dion's playfulness and her heart broke at the thought of leaving them.

She could feel Dion's tears on the side of her face as he continued to sob and say how sorry he was as he struggled to hold on to her.

As she felt him slip away she heard herself screaming "No, no," over and over as her heart cried out for him.

He made one last effort to tighten his grip on her, finding the strength from somewhere.

Janine felt her breath being taken away with such a huge wave of euphoria and she found it impossible to fight the pulling sensation any longer.

The last thing she heard was the distant sound of the band.

The last thing she saw was her boys laughing.

The boys had not seen how Dion used his free hand to take something out of the back pocket of his jeans.

They did not see how he put the twine around her neck as he told her over and over to keep looking at them.

They did not know that Dion had thought long and hard over the years of the least painful way he could take their mum.

They did not know how she had no time to fight as he tightened the twine round her neck so quickly.

They did not hear his final words to their mum, "You are coming with me," just as he had told her during their pillow talk six years ago.

They would not find out until days later that he had completely cleared his bank account of multi millions and left it to them.

They would not know as they watched Janine struggling that Dion had already arranged for his mum and Miles to comfort them and explain things as best they could.

No-one knew how Janine's life had flashed before her in her last elongated minute. As time turned slowly inside the sphere she remembered Dion's tears on the night before they left home in Cannock Wood and how he had told her. 'I just want to be with you', and asked, 'Can we go away somewhere?'

She now realised how carefully chosen his words had been.

She remembered his tears as he said goodbye to Rolo because he knew it would be for the last time; she realised why he had refused to take on any more concert dates for a while.

It made sense now why he had provided for the boys, why he wanted to marry her at thirty-nine years old, why he had spoken so movingly to everyone at the restaurant at the wedding and why he had said he wanted to spend the rest of his life with her.

Now she knew why he had smoked continuously for the last week; why he had been so drunk and wanted to make love so many times on their last night together.

She understood why he had found Jo-Dan for the band; why he had given the girls a more up front role; and why he made sure Miles was at the concert tonight. She now realised that Dion knew all along that Miles had been telling the truth.

Dion had planned it all – meticulously. She had trusted him implicitly, but there was never going to be a 40th birthday. He was never going to 'look good for' forty, fifty, sixty—

He saw what was to come as he lay in a coma, but he never explained it to her because he would never have got her to this place on this night and he never intended to frighten her.

He had never lied to her but he had been manipulative in the extreme.

Even those sessions when he had played about with her, holding her tight until she would say, 'I love you', had been his way of finding out if she would be able to break free when the time came.

She had been had. He had got what he wanted, just as he always did.

He had taken care of everything in his usual way, leaving nothing unsaid and nothing unresolved.

He had intended to take her from her kids all along.

A thousand thoughts had flashed through Janine's mind in her final seconds, including the scene when he told her, only this morning, he had signed over the house.

"We'll visit the boys and Rolo often," he had said. And as she was pulled away with Dion in her last moment, she had no doubt that he would find a way back. He always carried through what he said; that was her only consolation.

The audience and the band watched entranced during those final bars of the music as a capsule of sparkling lights encased the lead vocalists.

The scene became like pixels in a photograph, growing less and less clear, a quantum physics phenomenon which in time would be explained.

They could just make out Dion and Janine rise slowly inside the capsule, then disappear into thin air in a second as the sparkling lights cascaded onto the stage and fizzled out.

'Wow. What a great illusion', the audience thought. 'What a way to end the show'.

But there was more to come.

The crew, as instructed by Dion, released the giant new back-drop at the rear of the stage.

There was a roar of laughter from the audience as a huge picture of Dion was revealed. He was standing with his back to the audience, looking over his right shoulder with a mischievous expression.

His hair was tumbling down his back and one arm was raised into the air, rock star style with a defiant fist.

All he was wearing was a pair of jeans which were pulled down on one side to reveal his final message to the world.

Kiss my ass.

Thank You For the Ride – words and music by Dion

You hitched a ride and ran towards me
In my TVR sports car
I had started on my journey
And it seemed so long and far

As soon as my eyes saw you
And you sat right next to me
I knew just what I had to do
I couldn't set you free

Chorus
We talked and laughed along the highway
We sang, you said you loved my eyes
We made out several times along the way
I should Thank You for the Ride

We had many, many miles to go
I planned it all along the way
But how could I ever let you know
I'd have to make you stay
Chorus
We talked and laughed along the highway
We sang, you said you loved my eyes
We made out several times along the way
I should Thank You for the Ride

I promised that I'd take you home
But then I locked the door
I couldn't be without you, all alone
Wanted you forever more

Sorry to those who we left behind
I didn't know what else I could do
I was blessed with a determined mind
I'm going nowhere without you

Chorus
We talked and laughed along the highway
We sang, you said you loved my eyes
We made out several times along the way
I should Thank You for the Ride